TOMORROW'S NOT PROMISED

ROBERT TORRES

Good2Go Publishing

TOMORROW'S NOT PROMISED
Written by Robert Torres
Cover Design: Davida Baldwin
Typesetter: Mychea
ISBN: 9781947340084
Copyright ©2017 Good2Go Publishing
Published 2017 by Good2Go Publishing
7311 W. Glass Lane • Laveen, AZ 85339
www.good2gopublishing.com
https://twitter.com/good2gobooks
G2G@good2gopublishing.com
www.facebook.com/good2gopublishing
www.instagram.com/good2gopublishing

TOMORROW'S NOT PROMISED

ONE

In a failed attempt to block out the moans coming from the bedroom next to his, Derrick stuck a fingertip of each hand tightly into each one of his ears. Still the noises invaded his mind and ears. In the other room were his mom and some strange man. He had no idea who the man was because he'd come into their home while Derrick slept.

That's not to say they all came at night, because that wasn't the case. There were times when she brought a man in and sent Derrick outside or made him go downstairs. He hated it.

"Take this dick, bitch!" came the man's voice.

A loud slapping sound punctuated the words. The sounds were like the slapping sounds when he occasionally got a beating, then again his mother's moans. He hated it, hated the men, and especially hated the fact that his mom seemed to enjoy the acts. If she didn't, why would she keep doing it? Whore! The word echoed through his mind. It was what he heard some people call his mom. He had no idea what it meant and didn't dare ask her. He knew it was something bad. He unplugged his ears and swung his feet from under his Spiderman blanket. He couldn't block out the noise coming from his mom and the man, so he planned on sneaking out until the man left. The blanket hit the glass he had on the nightstand, and before he could grab it, it fell to the floor and shattered. Knowing it was one of the only glasses they had remaining in the house, he figured he'd be in trouble. He froze, hoping his Mom didn't hear.

"Stop, my son's up," came his Mother's soft voice.

"Naw! Hold up, shorty. Nigga, 'bout to cum."

Derrick could hear the squeaking of the bed a split second later, and then heard his Mom say louder, "Nigga, my son's up. Get the fuck up off me."

Unsure what to do, Derrick sat there with his feet hanging over the side of his bed. It wasn't long before he heard his mother's footsteps and his bedroom door opened.

Jocelyn barely stood five foot and weighed 124 pounds. When the two went out together, those who didn't know her thought she was his older sister. At just twenty years old having had her son at thirteen, no one thought she was a mom to a seven-year-old and had a daughter who was one. Looking at her, she didn't look like she was older than fifteen or sixteen at the most.

She stepped into her son's room, wearing nothing but the nigga's Steelers jersey she had snatched up off the floor and put on. The jersey covered her entire body, going nearly to her ankles. She looked at the broken glass and then at her son's frightened face.

"My cover hit it, Mommy."

She crossed the short distance to her son's bed. Taking care not to step on any glass, as a smile broke out on her face. When he fucked up or was bad and knew a beating was coming, he always came with the "Mommy" shit. Any other time it was Mom Dukes or he simply called her Joc.

She reached out and teased the end of one of his braids that was coming loose. She'd have to do his shit later. "See you up, young nigga."

He relaxed. He didn't get a beating that often, but when he did, they sure hurt. He only had a chance to nod and smile before the stranger appeared in his doorway.

"Let me get that shit, shorty."

She turned, not believing the nigga had come into her son's room. "Get dressed," she told her son. They'd be leaving right

2

after she handled this disrespectful nigga and got dressed herself. "Don't be walking into my son's room, nigga. What the fuck is wrong with you?"

Marcus smiled as he followed her. With her son being up, he knew it was a wrap with shorty. Some bitches didn't give a fuck about their kids. This one obviously did. He only met shorty two nights ago as he made a run. He was surprised to find out she was a crackhead. He had a baby's mom who stayed with him, but when he saw Jocelyn's sexy ass initially, he thought about kicking her out. That notion changed when he got to her crib and she told him she wasn't on no cuddling, lovey-dovey shit. If he wanted to hit, he had to come out of them pockets. It fucked him up only for a split second, and then he agreed.

That day he left her with two hundred dollars. He had no intention of seeing her again. He had no idea he also left her pregnant with her third child—all before the age of twenty-one.

~ ~ ~

By the time he was thirteen years old, Derrick got into numerous fights in and out of school because of his mother's drug use and prostitution. That built up his rep in the streets as a fighter, but soon he was recognized as a young nigga, down for whatever put money in his pockets. Two things he vowed to himself he'd never do: sell drugs and join the Blood sect of his Garfield community. With his mom's habit as bad as it now was, he despised drugs and the niggas who sold them. Gang members were almost as bad in his eyes. Both were added problems that he didn't need. Between trying to raise his two- and four-year-old little sisters virtually on his own, and school, he had no room for more problems. He got money the best way he could, lately by burglarizing people's cribs, taking their electronics and anything else of value he could easily get rid of. The financial part of their life fell on his young shoulders. The money his mother got from welfare for them went straight to the crack dealer. That was including the food stamps. Rent, clothes for himself and his sisters, food, and even the small birthday parties for his sisters were paid for by his crimes.

He had never met his father, and his mom had no brothers. What he learned about being a man, he learned by trial and error on his own. Yeah, at just thirteen, Derrick let it be known that he was indeed a man. And no one could tell him any different. Well, no one but Mrs. Anderson, an elderly black lady that lived in the same project court as he did, two houses over. She told him constantly that he was really nothing but a child—a boy. He always smiled at that. His child/boy years were long gone.

Going into the room his sisters shared, he shook the eldest awake. "Time to get up, sleepyhead."

Rubbing her eyes several times before she sat up, she said, "She peed on me again."

Coming into the room, he could already smell the strong scent of piss. That his sister now lay at her little sister's feet gave away what had happened. He hadn't planned on awakening his baby sis just yet, but now he was forced to. He shook her until she opened her eyes. "You snuck something to drink last night," he accused. His voice was firm, but he wasn't angry.

Tamika failed to meet her brother's gaze. She knew she wasn't in any real trouble, but she was embarrassed nonetheless. She tried not to pee in the bed and was doing good now that she didn't drink anything after seven o'clock like her brother ordered. Last night though, she'd been extremely thirsty and snuck some water out of the bathroom. She was busted.

"She be always peeing on me," Rochelle pointed out.

"Do not!"

"You do too."

Tamika, the more aggressive one of the two despite being younger and smaller, sprang at her sister, attempting to hit her.

Derrick managed to snatch her up before she was able to connect. "Calm your little pissy ass down and go get in the tub."

"Me too, 'cuz look." Rochelle turned, showing him the back of her nightie. "She peed all on my back."

He laughed—not because of what his sister said, but for the look Tamika gave her for saying it. "Yeah, you go too, and if y'all get in there and start fighting, I'm gonna beat both y'all asses."

They walked off together, and he smiled as he stripped off the covers. A big fresh semi-wet spot greeted him. It mingled with the dried yellow stains from the piss of yesteryear. He shook his head as he tossed the sheets and blanket down the steps. He would have to take them over to Mrs. Anderson's house since they didn't have a washer or dryer.

Stepping over the things he tossed down the steps, he went into the kitchen and put hot water into the mop bucket. He added the last of the Pine-Sol and went back up to his sister's room. After scrubbing the bed, he opened up the window and hoped it dried by nighttime. If it didn't, he'd flip it over. It wouldn't be the first time he'd had to do that.

Just as he picked up the bucket, he heard a loud noise coming from his room. He hurried there and found his mother standing there. At the sight of his closet door on the floor at her feet, his face hardened.

"Why you lookin' at me like that, boy?"

"Why you in my room?" he asked, although he didn't need an answer. It wouldn't be the first time his mom had searched his room for money.

Jocelyn wiped at her mouth and licked her cracked lips. They still remained chapped. At ninety-eight pounds, she looked like a skeleton. Her cheeks were so sucked in that upon seeing her for the first time, you'd think she'd just sucked on a lemon. Her hair, once flowing well past her shoulders, had fallen out from years of neglect. Her teeth, once straight and white, were a mixture of brown and yellow now—with several of them falling out or cracking from decay. The dirty shirt that fit her a few months before, now fell off her shoulders, as it no longer had any meat to hold it up. Baths were an afterthought as well unless she went out in search of a trick. Standing there looking at her oldest son, she knew she was busted and saw no reason to lie. "Can I have some money?"

If he had some money to give, which he didn't, he wouldn't give it to her.

It would only go to the crack dealer. "I ain't got none," he said as he bent down and picked up the door.

Begging or lying usually got her a few dollars, but that trick hadn't worked in a long while. Looking at her son's face, she knew it wouldn't work now. She left the room, hoping she could find something to sell once he left for school.

He hated seeing his mom like she was. He tried everything he could think of to get her to stop smoking crack. When the people from CYS (Children Youth Services) came to investigate them, threatening to take the children away, he thought that would be enough. She stopped smoking for about a week. Then she went at it harder. As the years went by, he gave up hope that she'd ever stop.

Now at thirteen, he stood five foot ten and weighed a solid 185 pounds. He no longer tolerated niggas coming into his crib to trick with his mom. Years of fighting had his hands right. And for any nigga he couldn't beat, the 9 he'd stolen out of a crib backed him up.

When his sisters got out of the tub, he quickly did both their hair. When his boys found out he did hair, they teased him a little. Derrick didn't give a fuck. The way he saw it, if he didn't do their hair, they'd go out every day looking a mess. So yeah, he learned how to do hair.

Once they were dressed, he took Tamika over to Ms. Anderson's house. She kept his baby sis for him. She never charged him what it was worth, but he paid her every week. Rochelle attended Fort Pitt Elementary School, and he walked her there next.

"Wait right here, Derrick. I got something for you in my locker," Rochelle told him once they arrived at her school.

She ran off before he had the chance to tell her he'd get it when school let out. He recognized several of the teachers—most of them since he spent five years going to the school himself. He had gotten into numerous fights there over the years, mainly because of someone talking about his mom being a crackhead, but early on for being a bum. He never had designer clothes and neither did his sister until he started buying the clothes himself. What he wasn't was a disrespectful or bad student. He was well liked, and the teachers who saw him took the time to speak and wave.

"Almost a high schooler, Mr. Wright."

Derrick turned toward the voice and smiled at the lady who said it. Mrs. Edith Dinkins was a black woman and also the principal. He always liked her. "Hi, Mrs. Dinkins. Yes ma'am," he responded to her question. Before they had a chance to say anything else, his sister tapped him.

"Close your eyes," she instructed.

He closed them because he knew she wouldn't show him what it was she had behind her back until he did.

"Happy Birthday, big Brother!"

He opened his eyes to see her standing there with a piece of wood in her hands.

He smiled as he read what it said.

"I made it in wood shop," she announced proudly.

The craft read "#1 Big Brother." She also handed him a card she obviously made that said "Happy 13th Birthday." He hadn't expected anything for his birthday. He was getting used to it by now. He hadn't had a birthday party since his mom had started using drugs, around age five or six. Receiving a gift on his birthday had been just as long. He hugged his sister tightly, "Thanks." He loved his sisters so much. He didn't know what he'd do if he lost either or both of them.

Edith watched the exchange between the two siblings and had to wipe at her eyes. The Wright clan was one of the many families she kept an eye on over the years. Since the crack epidemic, her job took on another dimension. She had to watch for signs of neglect. Early on when Derrick was a student, she called CYS and asked them to investigate. He often came to school hungry and dirty. Nothing had been done. She got word that Jocelyn still never attended any of the parent functions, and Edith couldn't recall the last time she saw her. The sacrifices Derrick was obviously making were commendable, but too much for a child his age to bear. She'd call CYS again that very day. He, along with his sister, were two good children. They deserved a chance in life.

"Hold it here until after school. Got to hurry to school." The bell sounded. "Hurry up to class. And no running," he added.

"Love you, Brother."

"Love you more," he told her, and he meant it. He smiled at Mrs. Dinkins. "Have to get to school. Have a nice day." He turned to go.

He only made it two to three steps before Mrs. Dinkins called his name. Breaking her hands-off policy for herself and faculty, she hugged him. "You are a very good young man. Happy birthday, Derrick."

"Thanks." As soon as he was down the steps, he ran down the city steps, taking two at a time. It was a run he was used to. He hadn't caught the bus that came up on Cornwall to get him in years. Arsenal Middle School was on 40th and Butler Street in Lawrenceville. It was his final year there and he looked forward to attending Peabody High School. There he planned on participating in sports —football and basketball, maybe even track and baseball. He had to excel at something in the hope of getting a scholarship. He had big plans, and if his mind didn't get him there, his athletic ability would. That was his only option. His sisters and Mom needed him to make it.

As he ran easily, he realized turning into a real teen wasn't half bad. Wasn't bad at all. He didn't know how wrong that thought would prove in just a few hours.

As he made his way through the halls headed to his first period class, he stopped several times to speak to people. He was punched once lightly in his arm. He smiled when he saw who it was.

"Twelve more," Denean said, and in rapid succession, she punched him twelve more times.

He rubbed his arm. "Your ass is getting heavy handed."

Denean Austin was a few months older than Derrick. The two were close friends, and since he'd given her a nice gift, a watch, for her thirteenth birthday, she'd been looking forward to giving him a gift in return. It was the first time they'd given each other gifts. "Happy Birthday," she said. She reached into her purse and brought out her gift. "Sorry it ain't wrapped."

He took the box and lifted its lid. Inside was a 14-karat gold chain and a cross emblem. It matched the one she had around her own neck. "Thanks." When he gave her the watch, he didn't expect a gift in return. It was nice though.

9

"Let me put it on you."

He gave it to her and she stepped behind him and put it on. "You getting tall." She was five foot two and had to step on her tippy toes to get it on his neck, even after he squatted down a little.

After it was on, he fingered the cross. It wasn't because it held some type of religious meaning to him. Derrick believed in nothing. It was one of the arguments he had with Denean. She attended church faithfully and had even convinced him to go a few times. The times he went when he was younger, no more than eight times, he used it as an opportunity to dip his hand in one of the collection plates. He dipped one too many times and was caught. He was forbidden from entering the church again, and he had to endure a stern lecture from the pastor. The man informed him that if he didn't change his wicked ways, he'd land in hell. Oh, he could have gone to another church in his neighborhood and continued his hustle, but that "straight to hell" scared him a little. Now the cross around his neck would have her trying even harder to get him to go to church with her.

The first bell sounded, and people lingering in the hall began to hurry to their classes.

"See you next period, birthday boy." She leaned in and kissed him on the cheek.

The kiss came as more of a surprise than the gift. It was the first time her lips had come into contact with any part of his body. Their friendship had spanned from the second grade until present. She vanished into her classroom.

"Mr. Wright, don't be late for class," one of the hall monitors said.

He hurried to his class and barely made it in the door before Mr. Gilmore, his English teacher, shut it. Still smiling, he took a seat.

"And the winner is, Denean Austin." She raised her hand high above her and gave her pageant wave.

The announcement had just been made over the loud speaker that Denean was valedictorian of the school. Derrick had come in a point lower and had to settle for salutatorian. If it had been anyone other than Denean, he might have been upset. He knew her teasing was just in fun. He'd been valedictorian at Fort Pitt, edging her out. They'd both be attending Peabody, and he'd get its top honors. He lowered his hand on his forearms as she blew kisses into the air.

"Hater," she said as she sat down and stole one of his chips out of his bag.

"Ain't no one paying you no never mind" he informed her.

"No never mind, Derrick. Listen at how you talk. It's no wonder why I always come in first and you are always second." She stretched the word "second" out as she held up two fingers on each hand.

They often studied together. If it wasn't at school, then it was at her home. It had been a long time since he'd taken her to his home. It wasn't because he hid anything from her. She knew about his mom's crack addiction. With her addiction getting progressively worse over the years, their home became barer. They had no TV, radio, or games. There was no living room furniture, just a broken-down chair and a busted bean bag. All the beds were on the floor, and his bed had the steel springs busted through.

Denean, on the other hand, lived in a home her parents owned in Stanton Heights. It was just a short distance from Garfield, but the two areas were like night and day. Not only did her parents, mother and father, live in the same home, but they were also married. That in itself separated the two areas. In Garfield, if there was a man and woman in the same house, the likelihood of them being married was slim. Oh, there were long-lasting hookups, but rarely did they lead to the marriage altar. Denean's parents were considered middle-class, bringing in an annual six-figure income. They had a two-car garage and went on a two-week vacation to someplace every summer— once even asking Derrick to join them. He had to decline because if he left, he'd basically be leaving his young sisters to fend for themselves. Yet he looked forward to the stories and photos of her many trips.

He was ashamed of how he lived, but they were close friends. "Here's to your t," he said as he lifted his hand in the air.

Having witnessed his salute a time or two, she gripped his wrist and attempted to pry his finger up, "Come on and lift it up so I can break it."

Laughing, he pulled his arm free. "Okay, I won't do it."

Before either of them had a chance to say anything else, someone from another table called out his name. Denean rolled her eyes as Derrick turned to see who was calling him.

Sitting around with group of girls who all considered themselves the PBs (prettiest bitches) in Arsenal School was Margaret Rhodes. She was in the eighth grade as well and was standing waving at Derrick.

"Hey, sexy," she said, causing the girls around her to giggle.

Derrick nodded his head at her. "What's up?" he was turning back to face Denean even as Margaret responded by saying, "You."

He saw the look Denean was giving him. "What's wrong?"

Since a few more of Margaret's friends came to sit at their table, Denean turned to face them.

Let him have her nasty behind, she thought to herself. It wasn't like he was her boyfriend. She never had one and wasn't allowed one until her sixteenth birthday—according to her father. What had her upset was Derrick was too good for Margaret. It wasn't because she didn't like Margaret—okay she didn't, but that wasn't it. It was the fact Margaret and the six other PB clique all bragged about no longer being virgins. To Denean, that was just plain ole nasty. If Derrick wanted someone like that, he could go right ahead. And in his own words, "It made her no never mind."

He shrugged it off. It wasn't his fault Margaret liked him. He didn't encourage her, and the feeling definitely wasn't mutual. One of his boys was hitting it, and he wasn't the only one. Last he heard, she was burning. Ain't nobody want her nasty ass. He thought Denean knew that. He'd have to tell her that. She got up before he had a chance to say anything, and left the lunch room.

"Come sit with me, Derrick," Margaret offered.

He ignored her as he got up, his food half eaten; he was no longer hungry.

~ ~ ~

"Derrick Wright, please report to the office. Derrick Wright, to the office please," came the announcement over the loudspeaker.

Hearing his name, he looked up from his social studies book. "Nigga in trouble," someone yelled out.

"What you do now, D?" came another voice.

Their teacher, a white woman, got to her feet. "That's enough. Derrick, collect your things. Class will probably be over before you return. Study chapter 23, and here is your homework."

He put his things in his book bag. Although Denean was seated right next to him, she still hadn't spoken to him since lunch. "I'll see you in last period," he told her. At the door, he paused and rubbed the cross she had just given him. His actions at least evoked a smile out of her. He left out, wondering what this was all about. He hadn't been in a fight for a while.

Dean Rush was waiting for him, and he followed her into her office. He didn't recognize the black woman sitting in a chair. He smiled at her nervously, because she smiled at him as he sat down.

"Derrick, this is Ms. Givins. She is a caseworker for Children Youth Services. She's here to speak to you."

He lost his nervousness and smile at the dean's words. Anyone, including someone as pretty as the lady in front of him, that worked for CYS was not his or his sisters' friend. They were an enemy.

Both women saw the immediate change in his demeanor. Rachel Givins continued to smile. She hated this part of her job. After working for CYS for the last twelve years, she'd witnessed every type of abuse and neglect. Prior to the crack epidemic, a lot of her cases dealt with a lot of physical abuse. Lately, though, it was a lot like the one she had now been assigned to: the Wright family—a case of neglect due to a parent(s) crack addiction. What she usually encountered was kids who loved their parent(s), and in those cases, it was heart wrenching to intervene—a sad situation.

"Derrick, our office was contacted by someone who had some concerns about the living arrangements of you and your two sisters. I went to your home, and after seeing the condition of your home, I've made the decision to take you three out of that situation. I'm sorry." And she really was.

He jumped to his feet. He couldn't allow that to happen. Not only did he not want to be taken away from his mom—he loved her—but he also didn't want to be separated from his two sisters. He knew that would happen. "Me and my sisters are fine. I take good care of them."

She had no clue if what he said was true. What she did know is at thirteen, it wasn't his responsibility to take care of his sisters. Besides, she'd seen their home. "There is no food in your refrigerator or cupboards. No television, a minimal amount of furniture, and your mother is addicted to crack."

"I keep food over my neighbor's house. A TV too." He had no response for his mom being a crackhead and there being hardly any furniture in the house. They both were true.

Moving them into a foster home seemed like the best decision. She still thought that and was about to say that, when he began to cry and talk all at once.

"Please, miss, don't split us up. I take good care of my sisters. I swear I do." He had to stop as he wiped the tears and snot with his shirt sleeve. "I work odd jobs to make money for the things we need," he lied. His eyes sought out the dean's. "Tell her, Mrs. Rush. I'm one of your best students here. Second academically out of everyone." He turned to look at Rachel. "I can be top student next year at Peabody. I'm going to do something with my life. Watch and you'll see. Just give me a chance. You just can't split us up. We are all we got," he concluded as he sat down in the chair and cried like a baby.

Both women wiped away at their own tears at the completion of his impassioned plea.

She thought she'd be able to find a home where they all could go, but that wasn't the case. They would indeed be split up. Yet after listening to him, she saw a slim ray of hope. "Derrick, you say you have a TV and food at a neighbor's house. Why is that?"

The look he gave her said enough, but he put it into words in case she failed to understand. "My mom sells everything to support her addiction—even food."

"You don't think the three of you will be better off in foster care?"

He shook his head vigorously from side to side as he tried to stifle his tears. "We are all we got."

There was a long minute of silence as the only thing that could be heard was the ticking clock on the wall and a phone ringing in the outer office.

"I know one sister is in school right now. Where is your baby sister?" Rachel asked.

For a split second, he thought about lying because there was no way he was going to walk out with her and let her split them up. He'd run first. The only thing that stopped him is she already knew where Rochelle was. If they ran, they'd all go together—even their mother. "She's over my neighbor's house—Mrs. Anderson. That's who watches them."

If what he said was true and there was food and things at the neighbor's, then she may be able to work something out. That is if the mom agreed to some outpatient drug counseling. "Take me to your neighbor, Derrick. We'll go from there."

He wasn't convinced that she wasn't going to split them up, but he realized he didn't have much of a choice. He took the tissue from the dean and blew his nose. He followed Ms. Givins out of the office.

After showing her everything and letting her speak first to Mrs. Anderson and then to his mother, he stood out on the walkway waiting for her to tell him her decision.

"Here is the problem I'm having with all of this, Derrick. You just turned thirteen today. Way too young to have all of these responsibilities on your shoulders." She saw the change in his expression and she smiled. "I know you feel like you can handle it all. And to be quite honest, I'm kinda convinced that you can. That is why I'm going to monitor this situation for ninety days. At the end of the ninety days, if things have not improved, I'll have no choice but to step in and do what I feel is best."

He'd sat in when she spoke to his mom. He knew what she expected and what the consequences were if they weren't met. Right then he was just happy. He hugged her tightly and thanked her repeatedly. He walked her to her car and watched her drive off.

Once the car was out of sight, he turned and looked at his mom, who stood in their doorway. He was so mad he knew that he couldn't face her right then. Not only that, Derrick had also already made the decision to do something he vowed he'd never do. In his head, he didn't have a choice. He started to walk, ignoring his mom and Mrs. Anderson, both of whom were calling out to him. He had to get his plan together.

Denean didn't see Derrick in 7th period or at the bus stop from which the two usually walked to her house together. Since he wasn't there, she caught the bus. After doing her homework and eating dinner, she walked the short distance from Stanton Heights to Garfield. She had to make sure he was okay. The surprise birthday cake she had baked and intended on giving to him after school sat on the counter in the kitchen—where it would sit the next several days. For four days, she didn't see Derrick. Every day was agony for Denean.

The close call with her children being taken away didn't put a ripple in her crack addiction. In the coming weeks since Ms. Givins had come into their lives and given her an ultimatum, the craving had gotten worse.

For Derrick, the walk hadn't managed to calm him down. When he caught his mom, smoking crack the day she was scheduled to give a urine sample, he nearly did the unthinkable: slap her. She cried and promised that she was going to quit. They were just words. He didn't see his mom for three days after that.

The ninety-day deadline was fast approaching. Derrick sat with Ms. Givins in the living room waiting for his mom to show up, but she never did. From the look on her face, he knew it was getting close to the time when they'd be taken out of their home. He told her he'd see her at their next scheduled meeting as though everything was okay. He knew that it wasn't, and more than that, he knew what he had to do and knew he didn't have much time to do it in. As he sat up in his room dreading what he was about to do, tears of frustration came to his eyes. He didn't want to do what he knew he had to, yet he had no place to turn and no one to turn to. When he told Ms. Givins they were all they had, it was the truth. He never knew his father or the three other children his mom told him his father had. His grandparents were dead, and his lone aunt, his mom's sister, was strung out more than his mom. All four of his cousins were taken away from his aunt. That wasn't a fate that his family was destined for. He had a plan.

While he sat up in his room crying, his eldest sister

appeared in his doorway. He'd just come from downstairs and had been home all alone but not now.

"What's wrong?" she asked. She'd never seen her brother cry.

He snatched up a dirty T-shirt off his bed and quickly used it to wipe his face. He stood up. "Nothing," he told her and tried to smile.

His sister wasn't fooled and neither was his mother as she came up the steps, prepared to go in her room to smoke the stone she just copped, when she heard the exchange between her two kids. She stopped and could tell immediately that her son had been crying. His eyes were red and puffy. Shame washed over her because she knew her actions were the reasons for his tears. Losing her children affected her more than she let on. She loved her children. She tried to stop smoking crack, but the desire to get high was stronger every day. It seemed to beckon her every second of the day, even when she slept, telling her that one hit of its potent toxin and all her problems would disappear.

She told herself that it was a temporary solution, but she couldn't stop.

Derrick hated the fact his mom was strung out on crack. He loved her though—loved her so much.

"I'm sorry, Son. I'm so sorry," she cried out as she sobbed. "I'll quit."

He'd heard it all before, but that mattered very little to him. He'd forgive her a million times before he turned his back on her once. At five foot ten, he towered over her five foot two frame. He pulled her into his arms and hugged her tightly. He felt his sister's small arms go around his waist.

Hearing the crying, Tamika also came up from downstairs and joined in on the family crying and hugging.

Derrick was no longer crying as he tried to comfort his

family. He rubbed his mom's back. "I love you, Mom Dukes. We're gonna be fine." It didn't feel like a lie coming out of his mouth. Whatever it took, he was prepared to do to it to ensure his family remained together. "We're gonna be fine," he repeated.

Hugging her son, Jocelyn believed him.

~ ~ ~

The two laptops he stole from an apartment in Oakland sat in the same gym bag he used to carry them out in. Most of the things he stole ended up being sold to one of the local drug dealers in the neighborhood. He stood in his doorway with the bag at his feet, waiting on the dealer he called to come through. He was nervous. Keeping it a hundred, he was downright scared, and it had little to do with getting caught. He wasn't sure if he'd be able to do what he had to do. He was scared of failing. When the truck he recognized as that of the dealer he had called pulled up, he picked up the bag and hurried to the truck.

"What's good, young dawg?" the dealer who wasn't too much older than him at age twenty-three asked.

Derrick gave him a pound before unzipping the gym bag. "Almost brand new."

Tre picked up one, lifted its lid, and watched it come to life after young D pushed a button. He didn't know shit about computers. All he knew was wifey had been bugging the hell out of him about getting her one. It seemed to be new, and the shit came on. "How much? Don't try to break a nigga's pockets either. I'll take one."

"It's a package deal," Derrick informed him.

He was about to say he only needed one, but his cell phone began to ring. He looked at it and saw it was a shorty he met at the club the night before. He had planned on hitting it that night, but his boy ended up getting shot outside of the club and he ended up being in the hospital the rest of the night. "Let me hit you right back, babe," He hung up. He was sure he was going to smash shorty, but he'd get her one to sweeten the deal. "How much you want for both?"

Usually he'd sell a laptop for two to three hundred dollars. He didn't know how much that would give him. "I want work this time."

The request caught Tre by surprise. He'd been dealing with the young nigga for a minute. He offered him work before, only to be told he only wanted money. Why the change now? "You want work?"

"Yeah."

"What's going on, nigga?"

There was no way he was telling this nigga his business. From what he knew of him, he was cool, but he wasn't telling anyone what was going on with his family. "Ain't shit. You trying to get these joints or what? Do I got to go to someone else?"

Tre stared at the young nigga a long minute. He never knocked another nigga's hustle. He was probably younger than D when he got into the game. Right now, he had niggas D's age coming to grab work from him. He knew about youngins, moms too, and that he took care of his little sisters. That's why he didn't mind coming out his pockets when it came to him. Still, he hesitated. "You sure about this?"

Derrick's face hardened. The way Tre was coming at him had him thinking the nigga was thinking he was soft or wasn't cut out to hustle. He had him fucked up. He took the laptop off of Tre's lap and put it back in the bag and zipped it. "Last chance, Tre. You want these joints?"

"Okay. I'll take them. How much work you want for

them?"

Derrick had no clue about that.

Tre saw his confusion. "Young nigga, you want to get on, I'll put you on." He pushed a button on his dashboard and then moved his arm as a secret compartment between the seats began to rise and then pop open. He took out a large zipper bag and removed a smaller bag before pushing the button again. The compartment lowered and closed. He gave the baggy to D. "That's an ounce of melt. Get your grind on, young nigga. If you want to re-up, hit me up."

Derrick put the baggy in his hoodie pouch, gave Tre a pound, and told him he'd get at him.

As he walked up his walkway toward his house, he realized there was no turning back now. He had to make enough money so when it came time for them to run, they'd have some money.

Jocelyn watched her son go talk to Tre and carry the bag out. When he got out of the truck with no bag, she knew he had some money. "Let me get some money." Before she could come up with a lie on why she needed it, he gave her a twenty-dollar bill. She was out the door even as she said a quick thanks.

He knew she was going to buy some hard. He had to check out what Tre gave him a little closer, without her prying eyes. He checked on his little sisters, both of whom were in their room, playing with the baby dolls he had bought them the day before.

He hurried to his room and closed and locked the door. He emptied the almost solid stone on top of one of his school books. So, this is an ounce, he thought.

It was April 29, 2006. That was the day Derrick's life turned around.

The morning after he got the work from Tre, it poured down rain. After dropping his sister off at school, he hurried back home. Not only was he not going to school this day, but also his mom was in the house and so was his work. He didn't want her coming across it.

His middle school perfect attendance record was broken, but it had to be. His grade was already in and he had passed on to the ninth grade. Getting an education and finding a good job was still his number one agenda. He hated the fact that he was about to sell drugs. Yet, he was forced to.

Despite not knowing much about it, he would put as much dedication into selling drugs as he did school. He wasn't totally naive about crack. He had friends who sold, and he knew even more that used. Transactions took place daily right on the block he grew up on. He thought about going to his mom and asking her to school him, but quickly nixed that. By the time he got home, changed out of his wet clothes, and retrieved the ounce he had hidden in the basement, he knew who he'd ask to help him: Ms. Walker, the mother of a girl he knew and an undercover smoker. Though it was widely known that she smoked crack, she always denied it.

He knocked on her door and waited. No one answered. He knocked again, this time harder. If she wasn't home, he knew who else to go to. It didn't come to that. The door swung open and Ms. Walker stood there with an angry expression on her face. He could tell he had just woken her up.

"Your mom ain't here."

Derrick couldn't help staring at her chest. All that covered it was a white tee. No bra, and her nipples were hard. He knew she was about his mom's age, and her daughter was his girlfriend last summer, and he shouldn't be looking, but he did before he could catch himself. "I'm not looking for my mom. I need to talk to you."

Now that she was up, the gorilla jumped dead on her back, putting her in a gorilla hold. She thought she had her habit in check. There were days when she could go without getting high. Today was different. The desire to get high was strong and the sad thing was she didn't have a dime to her name. Why did it have to be a little boy that woke her up? A little boy staring at her titties. Damn, if he was a little older, she'd fuck his ass for a couple dollars. She snapped out of that fantasy. "What do you want to talk to me about, Derrick?"

For a split second, he thought about not telling her why he came knocking. Then the thought of losing his sisters invaded his mind. "Need you to help me get rid of something."

What the hell was this boy talking about, and why was he talking in riddles?

Before she got the opportunity to ask him what the hell he was talking about, he reached into the pouch of his hoodie and pulled out a baggy. At the sight of the crack, her mouth watered. Quickly she grabbed his hand and pulled him into her house. She locked her door before facing him. "That real?"

He nodded yes, but held it up so she could see better. "An ounce of that melt," he bragged.

"Nigga, how you know its melt? You get someone to test it for you?"

"Naw," he admitted.

"Well, you don't know what you got. It could be some garbeno."

She could be right. It could be garbage, but he didn't think Tre would play him like that. If he did, Derrick wasn't going to take that on the chin. Tre would be dealt with.

"I'll tell you what," she began. "I really don't fuck around, but I'll test it for you. "

He figured she just wanted to get high, but he didn't care. He needed to know what he had. He opened the bag and broke off what he considered a nice piece.

Michelle looked at what he held in his hands and smacked her lips in disapproval. "What am I supposed to do with that small shit?"

He knew she was trying to play him, and he was no one's sucker. He let what he had in his hands fall back in the bag.

Seeing that she was about to fuck up a free blast, she stopped the bullshit. "Hand it here. I'll test it."

Without a word, he reached back in the bag, took out a piece, and gave it to her. She left the living room, and he sat down and waited on her.

Around five minutes later, she was back in the living room. "It's melt. You want to leave some of that wit me so I can sling it for you?"

He twisted up his lips. "Stop thinking you can play me. I ain't leaving shit with your ass so you can smoke it up. If you help me bag it up, I'll look out. Anything else, I ain't tryin' to hear, you feel me?"

Who in the hell did he think he was talking to? That's what she wanted to ask him. He'd always been so respectful when he came to visit her daughter. What happened? Now he was cursing at her. None of what she thought was said. The last thing she was going to do was fuck up a free high. "Okay. I'll do it."

"Ms. Walker, the last thing I want to do is disrespect you. Please stop coming at me sideways. I got to get this paper, and I can't let nothing or no one get in my way. Help me, I'll look out. Try to gank me, we gonna have problems."

Nothing about him screamed out that he'd just recently become a teenager. She'd misjudged him. Before she had an opportunity to tell him they had a deal, her fast-ass daughter stepped in the living room.

"Hey, Derrick. You miss the bus too?"

"Take your fast ass to school."

Kelly rolled her eyes. "Dag, I was just speaking." She had no idea why Derrick was in her house if he wasn't waiting for her. Actually, she was glad he wasn't waiting on her. She had no intention of going to school today. Mike, an eighteen-year-old boy, was meeting her at the bottom of the hill. She was going over to his house to smoke some weed. Derrick was old news and too young for her. Just last summer she taught him how to french kiss. Fourteen herself, she needed a man. She left out before her mom started screaming.

After re-locking the door, her attention returned to Derrick. "What are you trying to do?"

That's one thing he was sure of. "Make as much money as I can."

"We'll bag up dimes and dubs and take the whole zip to the ground."

He wasn't sure what she meant by taking it to the ground, but he nodded before she left the room. When she returned a few minutes later, she had a box of sandwich baggies, a board, and razor. He followed her into the dining room.

"Hand me that." He did. "Let's get started." She dumped the crack on the board.

For the next forty-five minutes, he stood right at her side as she broke pieces off of the large chunk and put it in the corner of the baggies. As she used the razor to cut the bag, she explained things to him. Like making sure to use the 4 corners of the baggie, not to handle hard without latex gloves on because it would seep into his pores. There was more she told him, by the time she had everything done. After she separated the dimes and dubs and put them in different bags, Derrick had forgotten most of it. All he wanted to do is get started.

Michelle cracked her knuckles and then stood up and stretched. Her head went back and her eyes closed. Her nipples brushed up against the fabric and hardened.

Unable to help himself, his dick got hard as he looked at her.

She opened her eyes and noticed his hard-on. He tried to use his hands to cover himself. Finally he had to turn away from her. Michelle smiled, thinking it cute. "You should make around eighteen hundred. That is, if you don't fuck up any of your money."

That was what he wanted to hear. The last thing he was going to do is fuck up his money. He knew what was at stake. "Where is the best spot for me to go?"

"East Liberty, down at the building by Babyland off of Negley Avenue. My girl stays in there and we can chill in there. A lot of snaps come through. Plus, you got this shit at the right time."

He had no idea why she said that. "Why is that?"

"At midnight, niggas start getting their first of the month checks. This shit gonna go like hotcakes at IHOP."

Music to his ears, and he couldn't help but smile at her.

Damn his young ass is fine, she thought as she felt herself get wet. His light hazel eyes, scxy lips, long braids, and white teeth had her almost forgetting he was not only underage, but her daughter's ex-boyfriend. "You want something else?" It was wrong to ask, but she couldn't help it.

He stared at her, wondering if he should tell her what he really wanted, but he didn't. "I got to go see Mrs. Anderson and make sure she watches my sisters. I'll be back, and then we can go."

Slightly disappointed at his response, she walked him to the door. "Can I have one?"

He gave her two before leaving out.

After locking the door, she went up to her room and reached under her mattress. Her hand came into contact with her stem, but she stretched further until she felt what she was looking for. Pulling it out, she lay on her back and pulled the shorts down. With a powerful thrust, she pushed the dildo up into her already moist pussy. Her body shook from the powerful orgasm that racked through her loins. Glistening from her cum, she stuck the nine-inch dildo into her mouth and licked it clean. "You like that, baby?" she asked out loud as though it was Derrick's young dick in her mouth.

Alone in his room, Derrick muffled his moan as he busted a nut into the towel he had in his hand. He opened his eyes as he wiped his dick and tried to regain his breathing. He wished it was Ms. Walker making him cum and not his own hand. Still a virgin, he couldn't wait until he got the real thing.

After getting himself together, he went over and talked to Mrs. Anderson, who assured him she'd go pick Rochelle up from Fort Pitt when school let out. He told her he had a job to do and he'd pay her later. It wasn't that far from the truth. He hurried back to Ms. Walker's, anxious to get started. They called a jitney.

T HREE

B y the time school let out that first day, he had $480 in his pocket. Every time he made a transaction, the rush he felt was similar to the one he felt when he broke into someone's house. Yet this was stronger. Instant gratification. He handed them something and they turned over the money. No wait or footwork trying to get rid of stolen shit. Money came to him while he sat in the bedroom and waited.

"Babe," Michelle said as she stepped into the room. "Some nigga is on his way up for thirty, and a bitch is trying to sell a Station and a few games. I told her you only want money."

He told her that after so many niggas came trying to sell him shit he didn't need: hygiene products, women's panties, kids' clothes, DVDs, and shit for the house. Now he understood how his mom got rid of the shit she sold out of their home. He had no use for any of that shit. But a PlayStation, that was different. He had played on one before, but he had never owned one. Besides, he was bored as hell. There was a television in the room he sat in, but there wasn't any cable hooked up to it. Right then a Station would be perfect. He handed her three stones and said, "Find out what she selling it for."

It took two minutes before she returned with the thirty dollars and a woman. She handed over the money. "Here you go, D."

He separated the 14 ones and 3 fives and put the change that equaled up to a dollar into his pockets. Michelle tried to turn away someone that came with all change, but Derrick let her know that if the pennies added up right, he'd take it. His attention went to the woman. "What you want?"

Her scheming mind set in as she saw how young the nigga was. "It cost a hundred and it's almost new. The games cost."

"He'll give you five stones for all that shit," Michelle stated, cutting her off.

Tamara cut her eyes at Michelle. Wasn't nobody talking to her ass. Was the young nigga her son or some shit? "It's worth more than that."

"Then sell it elsewhere. He cool."

Derrick really wanted the Station, and he was willing to pay more for it if he had to. He was about to tell Michelle he could speak for himself when the woman spoke.

"Damn! I'll take five."

He handed over the five stones and took the bag from the woman. Michelle walked the woman to the door, and Derrick took everything out. Madden! He'd hoped John Madden football was among the games. It was the year before's edition, but that was cool. As he began to hook it up to the TV, Michelle returned.

"Babe, you got to let me handle these slimy motherfuckers. They gonna try to get out on you, 'cuz you new to this," she explained.

He didn't have a problem with that. He already told her he didn't really want to see anyone. She told him how many she needed, he gave them to her, and then she brought him the money. It worked.

"Let me get one of them for myself."

He gave her one. He didn't know how many he'd given her so far. He lost count.

From now on, he'd keep tabs. Her ass thought she was slick too.

At her home in Garfield, Mrs. Anderson sat in her home watching the breaking news coverage of a killing of a Pitt University exchange student, shot dead on Forbes Avenue in an apparent drive-by gone wrong. The story was an all too familiar one.

Another senseless killing. The world was changing and it wasn't for the better. Having raised three children with her husband of thirty-five years, she thought she'd seen it all. In the eight years since her husband's death from sleep apnea, crack wreaked havoc on the neighborhood she considered home. She rarely got out unless one of her kids insisted, so having the two girls over gave her a respite from being all alone. But with the strange request to pick up Rochelle from school and then keep them all evening, she knew something was wrong. Having pizza delivered to her home and then a subsequent phone call from Derrick letting her know he was on his way had her waiting patiently for him. Ten minutes to ten, there was a knock on her door.

"Hey, Mrs. Anderson."

"The girls are sleeping right now and ain't no sense waking them up."

He had no intention of taking them home. In fact, he intended on asking her to keep them for the night. So, this worked out perfectly.

"Have a seat, son." When he sat on the couch opposite her, she said, "What's going on?"

The question caught him by surprise. He hadn't planned on anything but to check on his sisters and to give Mrs. Anderson some money. "What do you mean?"

Maxine Anderson saw no reason to repeat her question. She knew he knew what she meant. But she didn't need an answer from him. She hadn't been living sixty-three years and not managed to see a lot. She'd marched her way through the Jim Crow laws, endured racist home owners as she cleaned their homes for most of her life, witnessed the transition from Black Pride and a tightness of neighbors to kids no longer respecting their elders and each other.

With the influx of gangs, drugs, and senseless murders that peppered the city in every state, she hoped Derrick wasn't involved with gangs and drugs. She had that talk with him and explained the dangers. Yet kids were so independent and stubborn nowadays, that she feared he hadn't listened to her. She'd watched Derrick come home from the hospital three days after being born. Watched him grow up. Knew how smart he was. What she didn't want to happen to him was for him to become a product of his environment.

He hated lying to her. He looked at her like a grandmother. To him the truth was not only harder to tell, but harder for him to admit. He hated what he did, but he had no choice. He had already separated the money he was going to give her from the rest. He pulled out the hundred. "Mrs. Anderson, I can't explain things right now. With my mother on drugs, I am forced not only to take care of myself, but my sisters as well. I gotta do what I gotta do."

Hearing his words gave her her answer. No thirteen-year-old should have to face what he had to. She looked at the 5 twenty dollar bills he sat on the table. "You don't have to pay me anything for watching your sisters, son."

He smiled because he knew that. Getting to his feet, he went to her and kissed her on her cheek. "Keep the money. I'll be back in the morning to take Rochelle to school."

At the door, she hugged him. "Take care of yourself, Derrick."

He promised he would, before leaving. The front door to his home was unlocked. He didn't call out for his mom—just went up the steps to her bedroom to see if she was even in the house. Her bedroom door was cracked and the lights were out. He made out her sleeping form in the bed under the covers. Not wanting to wake her, he went into his jeans pocket, planning on leaving a twenty on the nightstand and then leaving.

"Where you been all day, Derrick?"

His hand froze in his pocket. The last thing he wanted was for her to know how much money he had. Finding her in bed wasn't that strange. The welfare check she was getting for him and his sisters was due in two days. It was like this every time the check was due. She'd sleep as though she was preparing for the three to five day crack binge she'd go on. He was used to it. "Out handling things."

She didn't like the sound of that and wanted to ask him more, but she didn't. "Is your sisters over Mrs. Anderson's?"

"Yes ma'am." He stepped further into her room. He immediately smelled her sweaty and musty odor. "They were asleep." He figured with him not staying in the house that night, his sisters would be better off with Mrs. Anderson. He didn't want to tell his mom that though.

In the darkness, Jocelyn nodded as her tears ran down her cheeks. She knew the truth. He was her son and she should be taking care of him. "Derrick, you are such a good son."

He could hear that she was crying. He leaned over and pressed his lips to her forehead. "You're a good mom too." He remembered the mom before the crack. The one who took him places, smelled nice, and rocked him to sleep when he had a bad dream. He loved his mother and he'd always love her, no matter what. "Stop crying. I'm going to leave you forty dollars. Before you go out, I want you to get in the tub. You stink."

She laughed as she wiped her tears. "You ain't supposed to say that to your mom." She continued to laugh.

Her laughter was music to his ears. It had been a long time since he heard it. He smiled as she sat up.

"Whew," she said as she caught a whiff of herself. She stared at her son proudly.

He was the best son a mom could ask for. "Thanks, Son,"

she whispered in his ear.

He hugged her back, left the money on the dresser, and went outside where he used someone's cell phone to call a jitney. He had to get back to business.

All alone, Jocelyn sat on the side of her bed staring at the two twenties her son left her. The demons began to whisper to her—telling her to pick up the money and call her dealer and get a blast: "Don't think about nothing but how good you'll feel after you take a hit. I'm here for you." She heard the words as clear as if someone was standing there in front of her. Her body trembled.

"No!" she screamed out loud. "No," she said softer as she began to sob uncontrollably. "No," she said for a third time. Just saying the word no gave her strength. Strength that she no longer thought she possessed. Her life, she realized, was in shambles—rocked by the craving to smoke crack. Why had she hit that pipe at eighteen? One moment she was begging her then boyfriend, who was a hustler at the time, to stop getting high off his own supply, and then she was asking him to let her hit it. He quickly loaded his pipe and sent her down an eight-year road of crack addiction. Her children, whom she loved dearly, were being threatened with being taken away, but that didn't stop her from getting high. Her life was out of control. She was out of control. But her beautiful son still loved her. As she dropped down on her knees, Jocelyn knew her getting high days were over. She thanked God for not giving up on her and rededicated herself to him.

After being on her knees for a half hour pouring out her thanks to the Lord, she got up and got in the tub. As she soaked, she thought about how to get her life in order. When she got out and got dressed, she set about cleaning the house. There wasn't much in it, but it was spotless by the time she got finished at four thirty in the morning. Sweaty, she took another bath before getting into bed. Before turning out the lamp, she looked at the forty dollars on the dresser that her son had left her. She vowed never to spend it. Her last conscious thought was how happy her son would be when he found out she was no longer going to get high. Their life could return to normal, or so she thought. Derrick's own addiction was about to kick in—the addiction to fast money.

He thought he made quick money before midnight on the first. He had to push pause on his Madden game so many times, he lost focus on the game. Michelle continued to come into the room until 5:00 a.m. when shit started to slow down. He wasn't trying to sleep there, but he wasn't trying to lose out on any money. Besides, Michelle put clean blankets and sheets on the bed after she washed them.

When she returned after making a twenty-dollar sale, she could tell he was tired. After being up all day, so was she. "How much shit you got left?"

Right before she came in, he wondered the same thing, so he counted them. "'Bout four hundred more. Why?"

"You got to re-up," she told him as she sat on the bed beside him. "It's slow now, but it'll pick up after mail is delivered, and another big check comes out on the third."

His earlier intention was to get rid of what he had and bounce before CYS stepped in. Seeing how much and how fast he made money, he thought about calling Tre and getting some more. He still had a little bit of time before CYS stepped in. Besides, with the money he gave his mom and Mrs. Anderson, the money he had spent on the food for his sisters, and looking out for Michelle and Missy, he was short of his $1,800 goal. "I'll hit up my nigga a little later." The decision was made.

Earlier, Michelle had her little cousin stay at her home with her two kids, so they were cool. She still had to go home. If she was going to be at Missy's all day, she had to get a change of clothes. "Babe, can I get a few dollars so I can run up to my house for a minute? I'll be quick."

He pulled a twenty from his pocket and gave it to her.

"Thanks, babe. Plus, hide your money somewhere. These niggas out here is foul. I told Missy not to open the door while I'm gone. You need anything?"

"I'm straight," he said before he yawned.

"I'll be right back." At the door, she stopped. "See ya, babe."

He liked the way she called him babe, and smiled. "Later." After he made sure the door was locked, he went into the bathroom and pissed. As soon as he came out, Missy was right there smiling her toothless smile.

"Can I get one?"

"Yeah." He gave her a stone and went back in her bedroom. He tried to get back into the Madden game, but his eyelids became heavy. Soon he was asleep on his back, his feet hanging off the end and the controller in his hands. Not even the constant sound of the whistle blowing for delay of game awakened him. He was out.

Michelle returned within the hour. She'd taken Missy's apartment key because she knew Missy wouldn't answer her knocks. High, she got on her paranoid shit. She intended on jumping in the bath at her crib, but decided since Missy had a shower, she'd take a shower there. She went in to check on Derrick. She turned off the game and the TV and took the controller out of his hand. A smile appeared on her face. He slept so cute, his mouth slightly open and a light snore echoing throughout the room. He was so fine she thought. Girl get your mind right, she told herself before she went into the bathroom and jumped in the shower.

"Can I get a wake up?"

Michelle came out drying her hair and jumped as Missy

spoke. "Bitch, you ain't been the fuck to sleep."

Missy sucked her teeth and rolled her eyes. "I'm sayin', he in my bed." Michelle didn't want to hear her shit. Crackhead bitch was all bug-eyed now.

Derrick was still lying on his back. When she told him she needed a stone, he reached in his pocket and dropped the remaining stones onto the bed. He never opened his eyes, and continued snoring. As soon as it happened, she thought about picking up the stones and bouncing. When he got up and noticed his shit was gone, he'd blame Missy's ass because Michelle would tell him she never returned. Just as quickly as the thought came, it left. Not only because she knew he'd continue to look out, but also because she didn't know what he'd do to her if he found out she took it. She took out a dime and handed it to Missy. "Shuttin it down to sleep for a minute. Your ass should go to sleep too."

She nodded her head in agreement, but she really wasn't trying to hear that shit. Who the fuck needed sleep when you had a full stem of popcorn? And that's what she loaded in her crack pipe, straight melt.

Michelle got high all day. Unlike Missy, who had enough and was ready to go to sleep. Again, she wasn't worried about Missy opening the door. Her ass would be stuck for a few hours, and that's all the sleep she needed. Planning on sleeping beside Derrick, she pulled him up further onto the bed. He mumbled something, but still didn't wake up. She took off his shoes and decided to take off his pants since they were coming off anyway. As his pants slipped down, her eyes stayed glued to his boxers. The imprint of his hard-on could be seen clearly. Here she was a thirty-year-old woman lusting over a damn kid—one as young as her daughter,worst yet her daughter's past summer love. It wasn't right, but she couldn't tear her eyes away. Vivid images of her earlier session with her dildo raced through her mind, causing her panties to get wet. Deciding to just take a quick look, she reached out with a shaking hand and pulled his rigid dick through the slit in his boxers.

The sight of him caused her to inhale deeply. He may be nothing but a little boy, but his dick was all man. She estimated him to be a size six to seven inches. Not small, not huge, but just right. Before she could stop herself, she leaned down and kissed the head of his dick. As she wrapped her hand around the base of his dick, they both jumped as one. She slowly tightened her hand around his dick and stroked him gently. With every upward and downward motion, she did, Derrick involuntarily raised up off the bed. Pre-cum oozed out of his dick, and Michelle expertly licked it away. As she tasted the salty and sweet taste of his cum, she was past caring about how trifling and perverted she was. She removed her hand and took him into her mouth as her own powerful orgasm rocked her body. In his sleep, Derrick moaned loudly, causing Michelle to suck and slurp on him even more. She gagged as he rose up off the bed and unknowingly shoved himself down her throat.

He was having the best dream of his young life. It wasn't his first sex dream, but this one felt so good. So real. Then the girl in his dream coughed. His eyes popped open. It was then he realized he wasn't having a dream after all. Staring up at him with his dick still in her mouth was Ms. Walker. He shook as she slowly raised up off his dick, toyed with the head before letting it pop out of her mouth, and smiled at him. Every nerve in his body seemed to tingle. He couldn't believe what his eyes were seeing, and thought he still must be dreaming.

Both of them tried to regain their breathing. Having her mouth on him, he wanted her to stop. It made him feel funny. Now that she had, he wanted her to do it again. He took his own dick into his right hand and began to masturbate.

Her pussy got even wetter at the sight of him stroking

himself. She stood and removed her clothes. Just in her panties and bra, she stood there and watched him stroke himself. Pulling her panties to the side, she stuck two fingers into her pussy causing Derrick to stroke himself faster. If he kept up, she knew he would bust a nut, and she didn't want him to do that. Taking her fingers out of her pussy, she licked them. "I want your dick in me."

He couldn't believe this was real. He envisioned her naked, but seeing her now went far beyond his fantasy. He couldn't say anything after she spoke.

She realized this was his first time. She could tell by the way he looked at her.

Her first time hadn't been special nor memorable, and she knew that she should allow his to be, but she couldn't wait a minute more. Stepping out of her panties and taking off her bra, she took his hand off his dick and lay down on the bed beside him. She pulled his arm, making him roll on top of her, reached down, and took ahold of his dick and put it inside of her. She bucked under him.

On top, Derrick shook and growled deep in his throat. He thought he was smashing her as she moved under him, so he lifted up preparing to get off of her. It felt so good when he lifted up, but it felt even better when she grabbed his ass and forced him back down on her. The noise she made caused him to rise up and pile drive back into her again. By the fifth time of up and down movement, he knew it was over. His body shook violently as he busted a nut.

Getting fucked by his inexperienced dick was a complete turn on for her. She didn't want it to be over, but she felt him cum inside of her. If a grown man had busted after five to ten pumps, she would have been furious. She wasn't. She pushed him off of her and then took his softening dick into her mouth. Too no surprise to her, it started to get hard in her mouth.

When she took him into her mouth, the sensation was nothing like he ever felt. He wanted her to stop, but then again he didn't. He put his hand on her head, really not knowing what he wanted—for her to stop or keep going. He got his answer when she stopped. His hand tightened on her hair, and he raised his hips, pushing into her mouth.

Once he returned hard, she took him out of her mouth and told him, "It'll feel better and you'll last longer than the first time." She got on top this time, guiding him inside of her. She'd be in control.

By the time she lay beside him, with a smile on her face and snoring contently, Derrick had the hang of the sex thing. He lasted longer the second time, as she said. By the fourth, he had her begging him to stop. Just thinking about how good it felt, his dick got hard again. Removing the covers off of them, he looked at her naked body. He positioned himself between her legs and then eased himself into her.

Her eyes shot open as he filled her pussy up causing her to have an instant orgasm. Her initial scream turned to moans as they got into a rhythm. He never felt so good, he thought.

FOUR

Over the next few days, Derrick and Michelle spent a lot of time fucking. She knew it was wrong, but she couldn't get enough of his young ass. For Derrick, the feeling was mutual. He gave her a look, and she knew he wanted some head or pussy.

Regardless of which one he wanted at the time, she enjoyed it. The one thing she wouldn't allow him to do is kiss her.

"My breath stinks," she told him on one occasion. "I don't like to kiss," she said on another occasion. Neither of which was the truth. She refused to kiss him because she smoked crack and didn't want him getting the taste in his mouth.

This day was no different. "Why can't I kiss you?"

She turned her face away as he attempted to kiss her. His lips touched her cheek. "'Cause I said so. Kiss one of them young bitches into kissing."

"You supposed to be my bitch, ain't you?"

"Am I your bitch?"

He thought he went too far and was about to apologize, and she laughed.

"Stop pouting, babe. I'm your bitch, and this is your pussy, but I still ain't kissing you." As she talked, she began to take off her clothes.

He smiled as she got down on her knees and took him into her mouth. His pussy.

He liked the sound of that. Before long, he was in his pussy.

She began to cry as well. "It's me, son, and I'll never go back to where I've come from." That was a promise.

When he was younger, he prayed to a God he had trouble

believing in, to get his mom to kick her addiction. That she never did proved even more that there wasn't a God. Now this. Just briefly, he thought God did answer his prayers.

After they collected themselves, they broke apart.

Most of his days he spent down at Missy's house selling drugs. He hadn't seen his sisters or mom in five days. He made sure Mrs. Anderson was straight every day even though she constantly told him she didn't need any money. He saw that his mom had cleaned up the house, but every time he stopped up his crib, she was never there. He figured she was out getting high somewhere.

This day he decided to stop up on his street one late afternoon. He knew Mrs. Anderson would be back from picking up his sister from school by then. He missed them and wanted to see them both. When he looked down the walkway leading into his court where he lived, literally stopped him in his tracks. He couldn't believe it and really thought he had to be dreaming. He stared at her for several seconds before he walked to stand in front of her.

Jocelyn laughed nervously as she ran her hand over her hair. She just returned from getting it done down in East Liberty. For days, she looked forward to seeing her son, but now that he was in front of her, she was at a loss for words. She even asked a few boys he hung with on occasion if they seen him. No one had. She was worried but now she could see he was fine. "Damn, boy. You acting like you've seen a ghost."

That's just it, it felt like that to him. As he looked her up and down he saw the mom before all the drug use. The mom he hadn't seen since he was 5 or 6. He said nothing.

His intent stare caused Jocelyn to blush. " I ain't seen you in days, can I at least get a hug?" He hugged her tight as tears fell from his eyes.

Jocelyn began to cry as well. "It's me, son. It's really me

and I promise you I'll never go back where I came from."

When he was younger, he use to pray to God that she'd get better and stop. His prayers went unanswered and that was one of the reasons why he never really believed there was a God. But now...had God finally answered his prayers? After a long hug, they finally broke apart and wiped away their tears.

For days she hoped he came home. He hadn't. "Where in the hell have you been? You better not be sleeping with one of them young trifling-ass girls."

He laughed. She ain't young, he thought. "Come on, Mom. Been handling things."

She had him and knew he was hiding something. She really couldn't fault the girls for going after her son. He was fine. But he was her child and he was going to do something with his life. Something more than be some tramp's baby daddy. "Come here, boy, and let me smell your little thang."

He pushed her hands away from his pants as she reached for the waist and laughed. It reminded him of the times when he was younger and she told him to get in the tub. He'd wet his arms, legs, face, and hair and tell her he got in. It wasn't long before she caught on. That's when she would smell his underarms and his privates. He wasn't small no more. "Mom, stop."

"All I know is no babies better not be popping up. I ain't ready to be a grandmom." She hugged him and had to look up at him since he was so much taller than her. "Thank you for loving me no matter what."

He didn't have much of a choice there. She had him and was his mom. He couldn't ever get another one of those.

"Let's go get your sisters. I got a surprise for y'all."

Together they walked to Mrs. Anderson's. His sisters were sitting on the floor watching TV. The front door was open. Derrick tapped on the screen. All three in the house turned their heads and looked at the door. His sisters jumped up as they saw him and screamed his name.

"Mommy is better," Rochelle said excitedly.

He opened the screen and hugged them as they noticed their mom was with him.

They hugged her as well.

Maxine Anderson came to the door and gave Derrick a hug too. "Where have you been and what have you been doing?"

"Ain't been doing too much, Mrs. Anderson. I been around."

She wanted to say more. He'd given her $300 in four days. He didn't win the lottery to her knowledge, nor did he inherit millions, so where was the money coming from? She really didn't need an answer from him. She'd figured out things on her own. What she hoped was she was wrong. Before she could say anything, music began to play.

Derrick reached into his pocket and pulled out a phone.

"Yo."

"I'm out and niggas is waiting. How long before you come back?"

He'd given her twenty stones and he'd only been gone a few minutes. Less than thirty minutes. "I'll be there."

Michelle sucked her teeth loudly. "Well, hurry up. Ain't nobody—"

He hung up on her not wanting to hear the rest of what she had to say. He put his phone back in his pocket. "Mrs. Anderson, I'll be right back to talk to you." He wanted to give her some money, but not now in front of his mom.

"Can I get a phone, Brother?" Rochelle asked him.

"No, and before you ask, it's no to you too," he told his baby sister. He took her by her hands and swung her into the air. Of course, he had to do Rochelle next.

Jocelyn watched her children interact with each other. She

knew how lucky she was to have such a good son. For the years she'd been getting high, he'd stepped up and taken responsibility for his sisters. For that, she was grateful. She knew something wasn't right. "Are you hungry?" she asked as they walked into the house.

He followed her into the kitchen. He opened the refrigerator and saw it was stocked with food. He couldn't believe it.

"The stamps came in," she said shyly.

It had been years since there was that much food in the house. Usually his Mom sold most of the stamps. He guessed she really was done with drugs. "I'll be back a little later Mom. I got to go handle something," he explained.

The surprise she planned was for them to all eat the homecooked meal she prepared. It had been awhile since she cooked a real meal. "What you got to do?"

He kissed her and bent to kiss and hug his sisters. He really wanted to stay, but that paper was calling him. "Something. I'll be back."

She watched him hurry away. Standing there, she wanted to call out to him, to forbid him to go, but she felt foolish thinking it. So many times, she said those exact words and left out. She feared that her son wasn't in the grasp of a nasty little girl, but a more powerful hold. They'd have to talk when he returned.

Derrick walked out quickly, knowing his mom wanted to get some answers from him—answers he wasn't willing to give. He went to Mrs. Anderson's house, gave her another hundred, and told her his mom was keeping his sisters. Before she started with her questions, he told her someone was waiting on him. He left the building for two reasons: to see his mom and sisters whom he missed, and to meet Tre to re-up. He hopped the back fence to avoid his mom if she was standing in the door, and went the long way to the street.

"What's up, Derrick? You ain't been in school for a while."

He turned and saw Kelly standing on her front porch. Michelle's daughter and his ex of a sort stood smiling at him. She had on a short mini-skirt and a matching halter top. Her pouty lips were glossed and her tongue darted out to lick a bright red lollypop. She was sexy; and he wondered if she could give head as good as her mother. "What's good?"

Kelly put the lollypop in her mouth and sucked on it teasingly, before twirling her tongue around it. She saw the bulge in his jeans.

"Wanna come in for a second? My mom ain't here."

He smiled as he nodded. "Yeah." He took a step forward.

Kelly held up his hand. "Wait! Go around the back. My cousin is here."

He hurried around to the back door. It opened and he allowed her to pull him in and then down to the basement. They went to the corner. As soon as she turned to face him, he pushed her up against the wall and forced his tongue into her mouth.

She was turned on instantly. She taught him everything he knew and was glad he hadn't forgot. When he ground himself into her, she moaned and bit his lip.

When she moaned, he thought of her mom, and that made him harder. He reached under her skirt and gripped her phat but soft ass. Their kiss deepened and he took one hand off her ass to fondle her tits. He unzipped his zipper and pulled out his dick.

Reaching for her hand, he guided it toward his dick.

Their kiss intensified the wetness between her legs. He played with her titties, but she yearned for him to take one of her hard nipples into his mouth. Lately she'd gotten into letting boys suck and kiss her breasts. And she loved the feeling. She squeezed his hand when he touched hers, and then she felt his dick. On first touch, she jumped and broke off their kiss. The boys she kissed always tried to get her to touch them, but she never had. Just from the touch, her body burned hotter.

"Touch it," he encouraged as he held it tightly, pointing it at her.

It moved when he took his hand off of it and she wondered how he did that. She reached- for it and held it. It was warm, hard, and so big.

Now it was time to teach her something. He put his hand on top of hers and showed her how to stroke him. Once she got the rhythm, he took his hand away. He had something else for his hand, or rather his fingers to do. He felt the moistness of her panties as he pulled them to the side exposing her lips to her pussy. He inserted two fingers into her. Her legs locked on his fingers as her body convulsed. "Open your legs wider."

She had to release his dick, as she needed both hands to hold onto him so she wouldn't fall. Her legs were too weak. She sucked on his neck.

He wanted to fuck her. Fuck her bad. Wanted her to feel how good it felt. He pressed his dick up against the lips of her pussy.

The excitement turned to horror when she realized what he intended on doing.

Panic set in immediately. She pushed her skirt down. "I'm not ready to go all the way."

He put his dick back in his shorts and zipped his shit up. "When you get ready to go all the way, holla at me. I'll teach you something, little girl." It was just a while ago when she called him a little boy because he didn't know how to french kiss. His cell phone went off and he answered it. "I'm on my way out, fam." He hung up, gave Kelly a quick kiss on her lips. and then left out.

She walked him to the door. As she walked up the steps,

she realized she had changed her mind. She wanted him to take her virginity. She opened up the front door planning on telling him to come back, she was ready. She wasn't a little girl. She saw him jump into a truck she recognized and watched it pull off. Why was he hanging with Tre?

"Who was that?"

Kelly shrugged. The next time she saw Derrick, they'd go all the way. She went up to her room and masturbated.

After getting the three ounces off of Tre, Derrick had him drop him off at the building. He'd have Michelle bag up a zip and hold on to the other. Shit went so fast he decided to grab an extra two just in case Tre couldn't be reached. With the shit he already had bagged, he served the people waiting on him. Michelle acted like she had an attitude. He didn't give a fuck. As soon as the last snap left, he gave a stone to Missy and pulled Michelle into the bedroom, slamming the door. He spun her around so her ass was facing him and reached for her button on her jeans.

She tried to turn back around. She was still mad at him for hanging up on her. "My pussy's sore."

He got her pants down, dropped his own shorts, and entered her roughly doggy style. "Whose pussy is this?"

She moaned loudly as he pounded into her pussy. Her pussy got wet instantly. "Oh baby. Damn! It's your pussy! Only yours, babe!" She began to back into him. "Fuck your pussy, daddy."

He did just that for the next fifteen minutes. When he busted a nut though, he envisioned it was Kelly's tight pussy and loud moans under him begging him to stop.

FIVE

He told his mom that he'd return, but he stayed out all night again. By the time morning rolled around, Michelle told him it was time to go home.

"With them big checks out the way, shit gonna slow up, babe."

He agreed. The majority of his sales that came in, came through his cell now anyways. He had an ounce and a little more than a half left when he packed up his shit. Every outfit he had in his bag was recently purchased from TNT Fashions, a clothing store in East Liberty. In his pocket was $7,800. It was more than he had ever seen at one time, short of a drug bust on the news. He left Missy with something nice and caught a jitney with Michelle up to Cornwall Street. They got out in front of her house.

"Am I gonna see you tonight?" She hadn't given much thought to how things would go once they returned to their homes. What she didn't want happening is shit ending with them.

"No doubt. You programmed your house number into my cell, right?"

She nodded. She didn't want to leave him. They had spent so much time together over the last week that she'd gotten used to him being around. She couldn't believe she'd caught feelings for his young ass. She had to stop herself from hugging him. There were too many people out on the block. "Hit me up."

He'd already given her $250 and some work, but he was getting at her because he wasn't ready to give up that good pussy. He left her and headed toward his house.

Walking down the street he grew up on, he felt like a different person. A week ago he felt like his life as he knew it was coming to an end. His main priority a week ago was education—school. He was far from a dummy. Who needed school when he was already making some good money, CEO type money? A person went to school so they could get a good job. Good job meant money. He was thirteen and in a week he made ten stacks or more. There was no turning back now. He walked into his house with a smile on his face. He heard his mom singing.

Jocelyn was in the kitchen at the sink washing dishes. A radio blared a Mary J. Blige CD that she was singing to. She had no idea her son had just entered the house, until he wrapped his hands around her waist, scaring the hell out of her. She screamed as she dropped the plate back into the soapy water.

He laughed and kissed the top of her head. "Hey, Ma."

She broke from his grasp, turned, and hit him with the wet rag in his chest. He jumped away too late. A big wet spot was on the center of his new Coogi shirt. "Boy, you almost gave me a heart attack." She turned down the music.

His shirt was ruined for the day. He'd have to change before he stepped out. "Where is my Tamika?"

"Watching TV at Mrs. Anderson's."

With his mom off drugs, they could start getting shit again. He really had stolen a TV and taken it over to Mrs. Anderson's for his sisters to watch. He'd let her keep it and go out and buy a few TVs. In fact, he'd go out and buy new everything. He smiled at his mom.

"What you smiling at, boy?"

He poured himself a glass of cherry Kool-Aid and put the container back in the fridge. "You look good, shorty."

She blushed. Despite everything, she felt good, like she had

50

a new lease on life. "Why ain't you been to school? Some girl came by here twice looking for you. Said you ain't been in school for a week. What's going on, and you better not say nothing."

"Graduate next week. I'm moving on to ninth. They ain't really doing nothing now."

He really didn't answer her question, but what he did say depressed her. She had missed out on so much because of her drug use. The last eight years were a blur, mingling from one crack session to the next. "Have you decided on a high school?"

"The Body, and I'm going to play football and basketball. Already talked to both coaches."

All of this was new to her. She was happy for him. She'd attended Peabody as well, but dropped out in the tenth grade. "Sit down a minute. I want to talk to you."

He ignored his phone when a call came through, and took a seat across from his mom. They needed a new dining room set too. Before either had a chance to say anything, someone knocked on their front door. Derrick jumped up, glad for the interruption. He knew his mom was about to ask questions he didn't want to answer. He opened the door, saw who it was, and blurted out, "She stopped! My mom ain't smoking no more."

Rachelle hadn't even said hello before he said what he said. It was hard for her to believe that. In fact, it was her last scheduled visit at the home. The mom had refused help and in fact slammed the door in her face the week before. Her hands were tied, and as much as she admired Derrick, she had no choice but to remove him and his sisters from the home. She even had a couple that were considering taking all three kids. She hoped she could keep them together. He had grown on her. She glanced over his shoulders and saw that although there was still no furniture in the living room, dirt no longer covered the floor as though it was carpet. When the Mom stepped into view, she openly gawked, not believing her eyes. This could not be the same woman from two weeks ago.

Someone with a long crack smoking history as Jocelyn Wright had, could not quit on her own. Seeing so many crack addicts told her that. Yet, here she stood, looking remarkable.

Jocelyn stepped up beside her son. She knew she was responsible for the CYS worker coming into her life, but she still harbored resentment toward her. This woman was coming to take away the children she bore. That's how she saw it. That was her crack affected mind. Now she saw it for what it really was. She extended her hand. "I'm sorry for the way I acted two weeks ago. That really wasn't me," she explained.

As Ms. Givins shook Jocelyn's hand, she looked Jocelyn up and down and then exclaimed, "You are gorgeous."

"I'm okay," Jocelyn said and then laughed.

"You stopped. How? When?" She paused, collecting herself. "I'm sorry, this is quite a shock to me. I just can't believe it."

"To be honest, Ms. Givins."

"Call me Rachelle."

"Okay, Rachelle. I can't believe it myself. For eight years, 365 days a year, crack ruled my life. All I wanted to do is get high. Everything else was not important, not even my kids. When you came that first time and told me I was in jeopardy of losing my kids, I didn't care. All I wanted you to do is get out so I could smoke the stone I had tucked in my bra." She started to get emotional, so she motioned Rachelle into her home.

Derrick brought two chairs out of the dining room so they could sit down. He stood.

"I tried to stop, but only because I figured with my kids

gone, my welfare would go too. It's sad, but true. I thought I'd never stop." She looked up at her son and reached out for his hand as her tears fell. "One day last week my son came in and gave me forty dollars, two twenty-dollar bills that I'll keep until the day I die. Yeah, I still got them," she said as she noticed Derrick's surprise. "They're in my wallet. Anyways, I was funky, desperate to get high, and he came and gave me that money. He hugged and kissed me and then told me he loved me and everything would be alright. That he loved me despite me being a crackhead. He loved me, despite me giving my body up for money and drugs. Despite me neglecting him and his sisters for years, he still loved me. That's all I thought about. It was then that I realized I had to quit. I haven't touched it since."

In her years as a CYS caseworker, Rachelle had dealt with and seen countless cases of neglect. Never had she heard an addict overcoming their addiction in the manner and as rapidly as Jocelyn had. If this was a long-term recovery, it was yet to be seen. She was happy for her. She was also glad it happened before the kids were removed. Derrick wouldn't have gone without a fight. He was a remarkable thirteen-year-old. A mere child. In a time when so many youth were running wild, being disrespectful, and lacking discipline, he was the total opposite. He was more responsible than a lot of grown men she came into contact with.

She explained that this visit was to be her last and that she had planned on taking the kids straight out of school. Then Derrick opened the door with the news. "This obviously changes things. I'll get with my supervisor and inform her of this change. With the exception of your drug use, there were really no other strikes against you." That was music to her ears. She didn't want to lose her kids.

Someone knocked on the door, and Derrick went to it and

opened it. He smiled. "What's up? Mom, I'm gonna step out a second." He did and shut the door.

Happy to see him, Denean gave him a quick hug. "I thought you was sick or something."

The mail slot on the door popped open, so he knew his mom was listening on the other side. He slammed it shut and kicked the door. "Come on, let's walk." He led the way from his mom's listening ears. "I'm straight. Had a situation at home that needed handled. That's all."

"You'll be at graduation at least?"

He laughed. "You just want to rub it in."

She brushed imaginary lint off of both shoulders. "A little sumpin' sumpin'." Some girls that they attended school with called out to Denean. "What's up y'all?" she yelled across the street.

His phone rang and he yelled, "I'll holla at you in a minute." He hung up. He had to get down to the building. He was missing out on money.

Nothing went unnoticed by Denean. Not the phone, clothes, or shoes, all of which was new. She was just glad he was okay.

Derrick was standing behind Denean when she yelled at the girls. The Apple Bottoms shorts hugged her butt to perfection. She was easily one of the prettiest girls in school. He just never looked at her as more than a friend. But after his experience with Michelle, he didn't look at any girl the same. Not even Denean.

She caught him looking at her butt and she blushed. He'd never looked at her like that. Other boys did, but never Derrick. It excited her, and his next words sent her to a place she'd never been. She got wet.

"You look good as hell. Gorgeous. You want to be more than friends?"

Her blush deepened, and she had to change her stance. She wondered if he knew she just stood there and had an orgasm. She laughed to cover up her nervousness. Her parents had told her she was forbidden to have a boyfriend until she turned sixteen. And she had a little more than two years until then. Her birthday was September 21. There were times when she fantasized that she and Derrick were boyfriend and girlfriend. Recently she began to explore herself sexually, and it was always with Derrick in mind. "You know my parents won't let me date until sixteen. They'll kill both of us." They liked Derrick well enough, but that would end as soon as they found out he was her boyfriend.

He didn't like her response at all. He looked at her dead in her eyes. "So you telling me no."

It wasn't her answer. He didn't really give her time to think. She rolled her eyes. "Dag! Did you hear me say no? Can you give me a minute to think?"

That was better than no. "Listen, you got all the time you need. I got to go handle something. Let me go tell my mom I'm going to walk you home." He ran to his house, hopeful.

On their walk to her house in Stanton Heights, Denean filled him in on what he had missed at school and the rumor that he was locked up. Both stayed clear of his earlier question.

She stopped at the corner before her street, not wanting to chance her parents seeing her do what she was getting up the courage to do. "I baked you a birthday cake. It's probably stale now, but tomorrow you are gonna eat a piece."

He laughed and agreed.

"This is good right here. Will I see you tomorrow?" He'd already given her his cell number.

"Yeah, just hit me up."

"Yes."

He looked at her and smiled. "Yes, I'll be in school."

"No. Yes I'll be your girlfriend," she explained.

A car drove by, and Derrick watched her wave. He waited and then he pulled her close. "Can I kiss you goodbye?"

It was her first real kiss. She liked it a lot. Breaking it off, she ran the short distance to her street. She waved at him. Her boyfriend.

He waved and waited for her to disappear down her street before he pulled out his cell and called the jitney station for a car. As soon as he hung up, it rang. It was a call from Michelle. He ignored it. Later on after he handled his business, he'd hit her up. She still had some things to teach him in the bedroom.

S_{IX}

With his phone constantly ringing and his late-night trips out of the house in the two days he'd been home, it didn't take Jocelyn long at all to come to the realization that her son was involved in the drug game. It hit her like a ton of bricks directly on her chest, suffocating the life out of her with its heaviness. She knew the perils of being in the game. It wasn't the life she wanted for her son. He was going to college, was going to make something of himself. Being a victim of the streets the last eight years, she could attest to its dangers. What she also witnessed is people who thought they'd sell it, only to become addicts themselves—many going to prison or making that final trip to the cemetery. Not her son.

On the third morning of her son's return, Jocelyn sat alone at the dining room table, drinking a cup of coffee. She blamed herself for his selling drugs. Just as she blamed herself for burglarizing people's houses. If she hadn't let him take on all the responsibility of raising himself and two sisters, he probably wouldn't have done either. What she wasn't willing to accept was this was it for her baby. As soon as he returned home from school, she would sit down and have a talk with him. One from which she wouldn't allow him to walk away. With her younger daughter still in bed asleep, she set about cleaning the house.

As soon as she stepped in her son's room, she noticed that he left a game on again.

She hated that. If you weren't watching it, listening to it, or using it, turn it off. It wasn't because of the electric bill. Being in the projects, she didn't have utilities to pay. It was just one of her pet peeves. She attempted to step over the controller wire, but her foot didn't go high enough. She stumbled, and reached out for something to break her fall. The PlayStation crashed to the floor, and she fell too. A pile of dirty clothes up under the window saved her from banging her head against the wall. She turned over onto her back, thankful that she didn't get hurt, while hoping his game didn't break. She sat up, prepared to get up, when she saw it: the panel inside his closet, all the way in the back on the side, was pried away. A plastic baggie corner was visible. With shaking hands, she pulled the panel away and pulled out the baggie. The bag contained a substance that she'd become all too familiar with over the years: crack. And from the looks of it, several ounces of it. Her worst fear was now very much a reality. But worse than that, it was a demon that a awakened a craving in her that she didn't know if she was strong enough to confront. Not since her decision to stop had she laid eyes on one piece of hard.

"Remember me, old friend?" it seemed to whisper to her. "I've been missing you. Wondering where you've been. Remember how good I used to make you feel?"

The tears began to fall. Guilt that she felt for her son getting involved in the drug game weighed heavy on her mind. One hit was all she needed. After that she'd stop, she told herself. She opened the bag, prepared to break off a piece, head over to a neighbor's that got high, and take one blast.

"Mommy," Tamika said, causing her to drop the entire bag, "what's wrong?"

With tears running down her face, she opened up her arms and accepted her daughter into her embrace. "I'm fine. Fell, but I'm okay." Her children meant the world to her. "Go brush your teeth, and I'll make you pancakes." Her daughter hesitated, causing Jocelyn to smile. "I'm okay." She really was glad the urge was gone. Once her daughter went off to do as she was told, Jocelyn resealed the bag and put it back where she found it. She couldn't wait for her son to get out of school. They had to talk.

The surprises didn't end with her finding her son's stash. At one, someone knocked on her front door. A man in a uniform holding a clipboard in his hand stood on the opposite side.

"Yes, may I help you?"

"Yes ma'am. Have a delivery for this home. Just checking to see if someone was home," he explained.

"Think you got the wrong house, sir. I didn't order anything."

He looked at the clipboard, then at the address. "Everything is right ma'am. 5336 Cornwall Street. Does Derrick Wright live here?"

"That's my son."

"He paid for everything this morning and asked us to deliver it. According to the order, everything in the house is to be tossed out."

She looked at the two large Freight Liquidators trucks parked in the street, in disbelief. Her son was doing things on a level she hadn't thought. "Do as he said."

By the time the men left, their house was fully furnished with all new things. The cable man even came to turn on the cable and Internet. They now even had a house phone. She used it to call her son. "Get home as soon as school lets out," she ordered.

He hung up. He was at the building in East Liberty, not in school. He kinda knew what she wanted to see him about. The day had come for him to tell her the truth. "I'll be back," he told Missy. He left out.

It took him five minutes to get home from the building in East Liberty. He had a friend's car that he rented for the day for five stones. He wasn't old enough to drive, nor did he have a license, but he made it home safely. He really hadn't learned how to park, so the front was in, while the back was out further than it should be. His mom hadn't explained why she wanted him home as soon as school let out. He saw the beds, chairs, and dining room table on the curb. He had spent almost ten thousand dollars on the things he needed for the house. His mom would have to go to Walmart to get everything else.

He stepped into the house and stood at the door and observed the living room area. Now you could tell it was not only a living room, but that someone lived there. He felt proud. I did this, he thought to himself.

"Sit down, Derrick," Jocelyn ordered as she came down the steps from upstairs.

He wanted to go look at all the bedrooms, the rest of the house in general. He sat down. "You don't like it?"

She loved everything, but this wasn't what she wanted for her son. She moved a pillow and took out the bag of crack. "How long has this been going on?"

He saw no reason to lie. "For a few weeks now."

She told herself that she wouldn't cry when she talked to him, but she started to as she asked, "Why, D?"

If she would have asked him that when he first got started, he could have easily told her the answer. Now he really didn't expect her to understand. All he knew is morning, noon, night, and sometimes while he slept, he thought and dreamt of selling drugs. It consumed his life now, the same way school had at one time. Was it wrong? Yes, but for him there was no turning back. He knew his mother was hurting, and he wished he wasn't the cause of her tears. He refused to go back to where he came from. He wiped his mom's tears with his hands. "They said they were gonna split us. Take us away from you."

She gripped his hands and held them on her chest over her

heart. "That's over with, baby. You can stop now."

He wished it was that easy. He didn't like selling drugs. When he first started, he didn't think he'd go beyond the ounce. It seemed like such a long time ago. Money was power. Made him feel like he was something. "I can't, Mom," he told her honestly.

"Selling drugs leads to three places: jail, death, or usage."

"You forgot one."

The look in his eyes she'd seen so many times in his thirteen years. A look of fierce determination. "What?"

"Rich!" he answered. In the short weeks he'd been selling drugs, he had made over ten stacks. Most of his stash was gone after he furnished his entire home. He wasn't too worried about that. In the coming days, he'd get it back. As soon as school let out he'd have all day and night to grind. By the age of twenty-one, he'd retire from the game a rich man. "I know what I'm doing, Mom."

She knew there was so much more she should say, things her parents tried to say to her when she was Derrick's age and the streets came calling. Her parents kicked her out at an early age. The outcome hadn't turned out too well. "When I found your drugs, I almost relapsed. If Mika hadn't interrupted me, I would have. CYS still isn't out of our lives. All I need is for them to find you're selling drugs, and they'll really label me an unfit mother. I can't lose y'all. I'll die."

He felt the same way. He'd never allow that to happen. "Mom, I won't do this forever."

"You can't keep that stuff here."

He hugged her tightly. "I'll keep it someplace else."

It wasn't much, but it was all she could do at the moment. "Lord, please watch over my baby. You allowed me to bare him, but now I place him back in your hands. Amen," she prayed silently.

Michelle was up in her bedroom when her son yelled up the steps to tell her Derrick wanted to see her. She jumped up excitedly. He hadn't stopped by often enough for her. Since they left the building, he'd only fucked her once. He came by to get some quick head, but that was all. The last time she gave him head, she had to practically beg him before he let her. Even when she sat down at the building with him, he never wanted to fuck. As horny ass she was right then, she was glad he stopped by. She was addicted to his young dick. Luckily, she had just taken a bath. She changed when he got there though, putting on a pair of tight shorts and a tee with no bra on.

"Hey," he greeted her when she stepped into view.

"Melvin, go outside and play while I talk to Derrick." When her twelve-year-old son did as he was told, she locked the door and hugged Derrick. "Missed you a lot, baby."

He smiled. He knew he had no other option where he could stash his shit. He was taking a chance, but he'd left her at the building with work before and his money had never come up funny. "My mom found my stash and she doesn't want me keeping at the crib no more."

She'd seen Jocelyn and learned through Derrick that his mom no longer got high. "What you want to do, keep it here?"

He hesitated. Would it prove too much of a temptation for her, knowing his shit was there? He really didn't have a choice. He thought he could trust her. "If it's cool, I'll get a safe and put the work in your room." His money would remain in his crib he decided.

"What you mean, if it's cool? I'm still your bitch, although you been ducking me and holding out on my dick."

He laughed. He'd been spending a lot of time with Denean. And when he wasn't with her, he was making money. "It ain't like that. I'm gonna go snatch up a safe at Home Depot. I'll be right back."

She told him she'd wait for him to return. When he came back, she had plans for his ass. He was giving up some of that dick, even if she was forced to take it.

The safe he returned with from Home Depot would be bolted into the wall. He bought the drill too. The pattern of her home was the same as his, so he already knew he was going to put it in her bedroom closet. It cost him $389, but it was worth it. He installed it while she watched him, before he put four ounces of soft and two ounces of hard, along with a scale, in the safe.

"Turning into a handyman," she teased.

He put the drill away. He'd keep that in his crib. He kept out a half ounce of hard that he intended to give to Michelle so she could get rid of it. When he got to his feet, his arm brushed up against her chest. He felt its softness, but ignored it. He was picking up Denean so he could take her to get a dress so she could wear it for graduation in a little while. Now that she was his girl he really didn't want to cheat on her. "You going to the building tonight?"

She hadn't planned on it. "If you want me to."

"Yeah. I got something to do. A few stamps are coming out. Make sure you have the address on each one," he instructed.

She smacked her lips in disapproval. This was one thing that they got into it about. Derrick brought the stamps only to send Michelle out to Giant Eagles to purchase food for all those who had children. And most of them did. He came up in a home where there was a crack addict for a parent, and he knew all too well what going to bed hungry felt like. He was losing out on money, but it was a loss he accepted. She tried to understand, but it wasn't easy. Some of the motherfuckers that heard he snatched up the stamps only to buy food for their house, took advantage of him. "I'll do it even though I don't like it."

He sat the hard on her TV. "I got to go handle something. Bring me back some money, but take out whatever you want."

She still had hard that he'd given her the day before. "Damn, babe. I hardly see you. Thought I was your bitch."

The look she gave him caused him to laugh and smile. He pulled her toward him and palmed her ass. "Stop trippin'. You are my bitch."

"Can't tell." It felt good to be held by him. She ground into him as her pussy got wet. "Fuck me, babe, please," she begged. She dropped down to her knees. Never in her life had she ever had to beg a nigga to hit it. Even now that she smoked crack. Her looks nor her body suffered because of her drug use. "Please, babe." She fumbled with his zipper and pulled out his dick. She didn't waste any time taking it into her mouth, her jowls stretching as it grew.

He wanted to tell her to stop, but it felt too good. Since the first kiss he had with Denean, the furthest he had gotten with her was sucking on her titties. She told him she wasn't ready for anything more, and he respected that. But his experiences with Michelle opened up his hormones, which he seemed to have no control over. Down at Missy's, he'd allowed Missy's daughter—a seventeen-year-old—give him head, and then he fucked her. It was a one-time thing, but it happened. As Michelle expertly gave him some head, his knees got weak and so did his resolve to tell her to stop. He sat on her bed as she continued to do her thing.

She stopped. "Babe, get naked. I'll be right back."

He watched her leave, wondering what she was up to. Denean hadn't called yet, so he had some time. He took off everything and waited on Michelle's bed, naked.

When she returned to her room, she took a moment to look Derrick over. He was a fine cocky nigga, lying there with a smirk on his face and his dick sticking straight up. She grabbed the remote, pushed fast-forward to where she wanted, and then pushed play. She began to slowly undress.

His eyes went from her to the TV screen, and then back again to her. Despite having two kids and smoking crack, Michelle had a perfect body. To him, perfect was a phat apple-bottom ass, a slim waist, a mouthful of titties, and no stretch marks. If she wanted, he thought as he looked at the TV, she could be a porn star like the woman on the TV. She had the looks and definitely the skills. She lay down beside him, and he finally saw what she had in the bowl: ice cubes.

She picked up one of the cubes and placed it in her mouth before she took it out and ran it across his chest and nipples.

Never having experienced ice on his body, he trembled at its touch. Moving it around slowly, she kissed him softly as the ice made a wet path across his chest. When she kissed his nipples and then started to suck on them, he almost told her to stop, thinking that was some gay shit. But then it started to feel good. Before long, he was pressing her head down so she could suck on them harder.

Using the ice as her lead, she took out another piece and popped it in her mouth to melt it a little before she ran it down his chest, stopping at his navel so she could flick her tongue in and out of its hole. She knew it felt good to him by the way his body moved. His dick hit her in her face and neck, straining to be touched. Pre-cum glistened on its head, and she couldn't help but lick it off.

The actors on the screen were completely naked. The woman was giving the man head. Then she placed his dick between her titties and pushed them together as he started to move. Derrick only had a second to wonder what that did for the man, before Michelle mimicked the woman. It felt so good he closed his eyes and went along with it. Every time his dick poked out past her tits, she stuck out her tongue, licking the head.

They switched positions with the woman getting on all fours and the man getting behind her and hitting it doggy style.

Derrick's attention was on the screen. He'd never seen a porn before. When Michelle took him back in her mouth, he literally jumped. Her mouth was cold, and he realized she had ice in her mouth. It felt funny, but good.

Michelle gave him some head until the ice melted in her mouth. She knew if she continued, he'd cum in her mouth. Normally she'd love the taste of his cum, but not today. She'd pushed two ice cubes into her pussy, but they melted. Her pussy was on fire. And the only thing that could cool her off was his young dick. She let his dick come out of her mouth. She licked and sucked on his balls. When she licked his asshole, Derrick stopped her. She smiled, as she realized he wasn't ready for that. She got on all fours and looked over her shoulder invitingly. His dick was the last dick she had had, so she was a little tight when he put it in. She moaned loudly.

Being in her pussy again, looking at her pretty ass, he wondered why he waited so long to hit it again. Denean—he knew why, but Michelle's pussy had a tight grip on him and she backed up into him. "Fuck this dick, bitch," he panted as he gripped her waist, pounding into her vigorously.

"Get your pussy, babe! Oh, damn! Fuck!" she screamed as her legs gave out on her, causing her to lie flat on her stomach. Her body convulsed mightily as she came.

He didn't stop as she went flat, instead pounding her and pulling her back up to her knees. He pulled her hair knowing she liked it. "You love this dick, don't you?"

"Yes, babe. I love this dick."

He seemed to go deeper, and all she could do was grip the sheets, bury her face in a pillow, and yell into it.

"Whose pussy is this?"

"Yours!" She came again as he wrapped his hand around her throat and squeezed just the way she loved it.

Just as he began to cum, he got a terrible cramp in his hamstring. "Awwwww," he screamed as he gripped her hips.

She thought his growl was because it felt so good. She went flat and he fell on top of her.

"I got a cramp," he revealed. He didn't try to get up, but rolled stiff-legged and gingerly off of her.

Michelle reached for the back of his leg that he was holding, planning to massage it for him.

"Stop," he ordered, as he was afraid of her touch. The shit really hurt. As soon as the pain began to subside, he attempted to stand, and the pain came back double. He fell back onto the bed, gripping his leg.

She tried not to laugh, but couldn't stop herself. The look on his face, grimacing in pain, was hilarious to her. Seeing he didn't like her laughing, she turned over on her stomach and buried her head into the pillow.

The pain in his leg was hurting. He didn't see what the fuck she thought was funny. When she rolled onto her stomach, he decided to see how funny it was when she was hurting. He raised his hand and brought it down hard on her phat ass. The sound was nothing near as loud as her scream. She flipped over, an angry expression on her face. "Ain't shit funny now, is it?"

Tears ran down her cheeks. She continued to rub her butt trying to take the sting out of it. "I ain't do shit to your leg, Derrick."

He finally managed to stand. He reached out attempting to touch her, but she wasn't feeling him right then, and rolled out of his reach. He laughed as he got dressed. Once he was dressed, he took out his roll of money and put two hundred on the dresser. "Go out and snatch up some sexy shit so I can tear it off of you." He'd seen that on the porn DVD.

She was falling in love with the young nigga. She didn't want him to know that, but she was. She would go get some things from Frederick's of Hollywood.

He left her in her room and walked down the steps.

Kelly had entered her home and heard the moans coming through the floor. Her mom had company, and from all the noise, the nigga was working with something, because he had her mom moaning. Standing there, Kelly's panties got wet. Her experience with boys had grown. She'd even allowed someone to lick her. It felt good. She'd go all the way soon, and then she'd get Derrick to come over and put it on him.

Derrick planned on going home and jumping in the shower. He didn't want Denean to smell sex on him. He nearly ran into Kelly. He smiled. He hoped she had just come in and hadn't heard him and her Mom. "What's up?"

She couldn't believe Derrick was upstairs with her mother. She'd been trying to get up the nerve to go all the way with him. She was going to do it, and now this. Tears began to fall from her eyes. She ran out of the room and up the stairs. A door slammed.

Derrick didn't want to hurt Kelly. She had obviously heard him and her mom. He was going to go up and talk to her or at least tell Michelle that she overheard them, but his phone rang. "Hey, gorgeous," he answered.

"Waiting on you, sexy," Denean told him.

"I'll be there in twenty minutes." He hung up. He'd talk to Kelly later. For now he still had to get in the tub, so he left out.

Up in her bedroom, Kelly cried, ignoring her mom's knocks. She hated her nasty ass, hated her and hated Derrick.

SEVEN

The summer swept by for Derrick. As predicted, he made a lot of money. By the time Peabody High School started and he began the ninth grade, he knew selling drugs was what he was destined to do. When his phone rang, regardless of which class he was in, he stepped out to answer it. He missed a lot of the first two weeks of classes, attracting the attention of the ninth-grade guidance counselor. He was told that he was wanted in her office. He got that message at the same time he got a call on his phone for a hundred dollars. It took him twenty minutes to finally make it to her office.

He took a seat in her office and looked across the desk at the middle-aged white woman as she finished up the call she was on. His phone vibrated, but he ignored it cause she hung up and smiled at him.

"Mr. Wright, my name is Charlene Knox-Timmons. I am the ninth-grade counselor. It's been brought to my attention that you've missed a lot of days of school, and even when you are here, you leave at times in the middle of class. Can you tell me what's going on?"

He doubted she wanted to hear what he'd been doing, especially in the last few days, since it was the beginning of the month. Too much money to be made to worry about school.

"Is it your home situation?" she asked before he had a chance to answer. She'd reviewed his file and knew of his mother's drug use. "Is something going on there?"

The question got his attention and caused him to sit up straighter. "Ain't shit wrong with my home situation." They'd just gotten out from under CYS's watch. His mom became friends with Rachelle Givins, and the two often talked on the phone or went out together. Derrick knew they were only a phone call away from CYS stepping in again. It wasn't going to be because of some shit he did.

"Mr. Wright, there is no need to use profanity. I'm here to help you." Her face turned red as she spoke.

He thought he could juggle selling drugs and school, but knew that he couldn't. Fiends don't stop getting high during school hours. Michelle still held him down most days by going to the building for him. The problem was, most of his sales came through his cell phone. He had to get shit together. He smiled. "I'm sorry, Mrs. Timmons. Still adjusting. I'll get it together," he informed her. Getting an education was still a priority for him. Once he was rich, and he would be, he'd have to be smart enough to keep it.

Maybe he would still go on to college once he got out of the game. After his recent talk with Denean, going to college and focusing on school was becoming important again. She hadn't issued an ultimatum, but she said, "I'm not doing the jail shit, Derrick. No visits, letters, nothing. You're selling drugs and you don't have to."

Twice in a matter of twenty-four hours someone had come at his neck about hustling. Add his mom's consistent nagging, and it was three.

"Well, I'm here to help you. Any time you need to talk, I'm only a knock away."

He got to his feet. "Thanks, Mrs. Timmons." He left her office and hurried to his next class. Denean was in that class with him. He hadn't seen her for three classes.

As soon as the final bell rang, he grabbed up his bag and hurried out of the class. He decided to rededicate himself to school. From fourth period to the final bell, he didn't answered one call. Not even Michelle's. He had a total of thirty-four missed calls. He listened to his messages as he weaved his way through people trying to hurry. Denean said she'd meet him at the front door. He hoped she was there waiting on him. Michelle accused him in her message of being with a bitch and told him he'd find her at her house. He had forgotten to see her before school, and she ran out of work. More money lost.

"Big baller, when you gonna let a nigga on your team?" the brown-skinned boy asked.

Aaron Rodgers, age sixteen, walked up to Derrick and gave him a pound.

Derrick smiled. "Barely making it myself, fam," he told the dude he knew from Garfield.

"Fam, we both know that's some bullshit." He lowered his voice and leaned closer and whispered, "My connect got bullshit. Heard you got melt."

Despite being in the game for several months, Derrick still took his shit to the ground. Tre and Michelle both encouraged him to start getting rid of weight. The way he figured, he'd be losing out on money by selling weight. It wasn't the first time someone came at him wanting weight. He turned them all down. As he stood there, he had the solution to his problem. "Holla at me in a minute. Got to drop my girl off at home."

"Real talk?"

Derrick nodded yes. He saw Denean, made his way to her, and kissed her lightly on her lips.

"Hey, sexy. Hi, Aaron," she said speaking to them both.

"Miss me, gorgeous?" Derrick said.

She held her thumb and index finger merely apart and said, "This much."

He hugged her, wrapping his arm around her waist as she laughed. "Holla at me," he told Aaron as he walked out with his woman at his side.

Despite both of them being freshmen, the two were not only

known, but also envied. Word spread that Derrick was making some serious paper on the low, and Denean had him. Their walk was made longer because they had to stop and greet so many different people. Finally, they made it to the back of the school where Derrick always parked his '98 Monte Carlo SS because he wasn't even fourteen yet. He was still a year from even being allowed to get a permit to drive around with a licensed driver. There was real po-po in the school, so he paid the lady who lived at the house he parked in front of to watch his shit. The car cost nine stacks and was in Michelle's name. He got in, rolled down the windows, and cranked up the system. Blasting Lil Wayne's "Bo DJ," he drove past his classmates and teachers. Life couldn't be better for them.

Neither knew the storm that was slowly blowing their way—a storm that would change their young lives forever.

Selling weight instead of grinding everything to the ground opened up a whole new dimension in the game for Derrick. He thought he'd lose out on so much money, but in actuality, he ended up making more. He still copped from Tre, but instead of getting his work already cooked, he snatched up soft and learned the craft of cooking up from Shelly Thunder and Gator. They were two seasoned crack users from Garfield, who could cook up a whole bird in a little more than an hour. They didn't steal and they didn't lose much. They were two people he could trust, caught up on the wrong side of the game. By October, he'd built up a nice clientele and worked at his schooling. His money was straight, and it appeared he had no worries.

Then the storms began. With his name ringing bells in the streets, it wasn't long before someone sought out to test him. At first, they came at him in school, where he had to show on two different occasions that his hands were a sufficient weapon. And then one night when he got in from a late night out, two niggas in black tried to run up on him when he got out of his car on Cornwall. He let his 9 do the talking, leaving one nigga bleeding in the street and the other hightailing it over a fence and down the hillside. His rep in the streets was cemented after that. Shit changed him as he knew it would.

Even Denean, who was nice to everyone, got tested. She had to show bitches she wasn't with the disrespect and bullshit. It happened one day in the lunch room when a senior girl stopped at the table Denean was sitting at with Derrick and a few more junior varsity football players and cheerleaders, and mindless of Denean sitting there, tapped Derrick on the shoulder.

"When you get tired of fucking with little girls and want to upgrade baby, get at me."

The paper she extended to him never reached his hands. Without uttering a word, Denean was up and commenced to beat the black off of the girl. Her nice girl image took a major hit that day, and she got suspended for the first time in her life. The dislike her father now harbored for Derrick magnified that day as well.

Upset that she had a boyfriend before her sixteenth birthday to a boy involved in the streets ate at her father. He didn't like it, and he didn't like Derrick. He forbade Denean from seeing him, and Derrick was no longer welcome his home. That didn't stop them from seeing each other. After the fight, Denean was grounded, but she saw him in school once her three-day suspension ended.

The two were boyfriend and girlfriend in every sense of the word, except sex.

October 20, 2006, all that would change.

"Don't make no plans for today. I have something special planned," Denean told Derrick during first period.

He'd said those same words to her on September 27, her birthday, the month before. He didn't have any plans for today, anyway. He had football practice after school, but that was it.

After practice, he walked off the field arm in arm with Denean, who had been sitting in the stands watching him. The cheerleaders, which she was a part of, didn't hold practice that day.

His sisters decorated the living room and baked him a cake for a small family party. He could tell something was on Denean's mind, because she was quiet and nervous during it all. When he questioned her, she told him she was cool. He didn't press her.

It was around seven thirty at night when they left. He'd shown Denean how to drive, and she was behind the wheel now.

"I can tell something is wrong, gorgeous. You ain't gonna tell me?"

She pulled over to the side of the road, cut off the car, and turned to look at him. "I want you to answer something for me honestly, Derrick."

He always kept it a hundred with her. "Okay."

"Do you love me?"

He laughed, but he could tell she was serious. "You really need me to answer that?"

She was about to make the biggest decision in her life—one that she could never take back, correct or undue. It was a question she needed an answer to. "Yes."

Every single day he tried to show her how much he loved her. "Gorgeous, you are my heart. I love you without a doubt. I put that on the dead homies."

Looking into his eyes, she could tell he was keeping it a hundred. For him to put it on all his homies that were killed or died cemented it all for her. She reached into her purse and withdrew the hard piece of plastic that resembled a credit card, and placed it in his hands. "I love you, sexy, and I'm ready to take our relationship to another level. My birthday gift to you, is myself."

He'd been wanting her for awhile now, but he wasn't going to pressure her. Now that the time was here, he couldn't believe it.

"We got valet parking. Come upstairs in twenty minutes. I got to go get everything ready." She leaned in and kissed him passionately. It left them both yearning for more. "Twenty minutes," she said before getting out.

This is it, she thought as she walked into the hotel in Shadyside—the Marriott. Since she was too young, Denean got her twenty-two-year-old cousin to get the room for her. She also asked for her advice.

Precious had lost her virginity to her no-good dirty-ass neighbor on the basement floor on a pile of dirty clothes at the age of twelve. He had been fifteen. There wasn't anything special or memorable about the encounter that lasted all of five minutes—if that long. If she had to do it all over again, she would have chosen a better partner and better setting. Probably even waited until she was older. After making sure her little cousin was positive this was what she wanted to do, she gave in. Besides, she really liked Derrick. The two were perfect for each other.

"Touching," she said as they rode to Victoria's Secret store in Monroeville Mall. "This is the most important part. You don't want him to get on top of you and hump a mile a minute. Is he a virgin too?"

"No."

She could tell the way her cousin said it that she wasn't happy about it. "Lil cuz, don't sweat that. The last thing you want is an inexperienced lover your first time. That's nothing nice." Then she began to tell her in graphic detail what to do.

Some things her cousin told her, Denean didn't know if she

was up for. As they parked in the mall parking lot, Denean wanted to know one thing: "Is it going to hurt a lot?"

Precious smiled. "Yeah, more so if he's working with something. But by the second and third time, if you are lucky enough to go that far tonight, the pleasure will outweigh the pain."

As she stood in the room after taking a quick shower and putting on the Victoria's Secret lace outfit, she hoped her cousin was right.

Exactly twenty minutes later, the door to the room opened and she watched him step into the room. She stood at the foot of the bed by the TV. The lights were out, but the room was illuminated by the fourteen candles placed in various parts of the room.

Derrick locked the door and stood there a long moment staring at her. "Happy birthday, sexy."

They came together as though they were one.

One night wasn't enough for either of them. Derrick paid for another night and they spent it exploring each other's bodies. By the second day and night, they eclipsed the second or third time Precious said it would take for it to start to be enjoyable, and on that she hadn't lied. Denean loved giving herself to Derrick.

They missed school, and Denean failed to tell her parents she was staying at her cousin Precious's house. Her cousin covered for her. Though a month after their hotel stay, Denean missed her period. After buying a pregnancy test from Rite-Aid, she got confirmation that despite using condoms every single time, she was pregnant.

"Bitch, for real," Amber, "Mutter" to all her friends, Goodwyn exclaimed in disbelief. If one of her other friends had revealed the same news as her best friend, Denean, she wouldn't have had a problem with it. But Denean knocked?

"You sure you're pregnant?"

"Shhhhhh!" Denean's parents were in the house, and she didn't want them to know. Not now. Not ever. Mutter's big mouth could easily be overheard.

"My bad. Damn!"

It was worthy of more than a "damn" in Denean's eyes. She was royally fucked.

She pulled out both pregnancy sticks to show her friend.

Mutter had taken a test herself before, so she knew how to read one. She was fourteen months older than Denean, and the two had been friends since they were eight and nine respectively and attended Big Brother/Big Sister together. She got the heads-up that her girl was sexually active now. She also knew her girl was smart enough to use condoms. "Does D know?"

Denean shook her head no. "Plan on telling him tonight."

"You want me there?" Denean was there when Mutter spoke to the doctor about getting an abortion. She'd be there for her girl.

It wasn't Derrick she was worried about. He loved her. They hadn't spoken about having a baby together, but she didn't think he'd be on some funny shit. The dude Mutter got knocked up by told her it wasn't his and he didn't want anything to do with her. True to his word, he stopped coming around. "I'll be cool."

"Can I rock these?"

The earrings Mutter held up to her ears were a gift from Derrick. Those things were usually off-limits to anyone, but Denean was preoccupied with her situation. "Bring 'em back."

Mutter took out the ones in her ears and replaced them with the ones she just borrowed. She modeled them in the mirror and then asked, "When are you going to tell your parents?"

Denean had no idea and really didn't want to think about

that. She began to get a headache.

Since his relationship with Denean went to the next level, Derrick had toned down shit with Michelle. She still went down to the building whenever he asked her to, and he still kept his work at her crib, but with the exception of getting some head from her once, the sex shit was a wrap for them—a fact Michelle didn't like at all.

Derrick bought her a table and a swivel chair to go in her bedroom, that he used to sit at to weigh and bag up his work. Usually they'd talk while he did this, but this time no words were spoken by the two. Michelle sat on the bed, and he could tell by the look on her face that something was on her mind. He kinda guessed it had a lot to do with the fact that he was no longer sexing her, but he truly just wanted Denean. The last thing he wanted to do was hurt Michelle. Since he got into the game, she'd held him down. He'd give her something extra once he bounced. Unable to take the silence any longer, he picked up the remote off the bed and turned the TV on. The regular station came in. Figuring he had it on the wrong station for cable, he switched it to 3. "What's up with the cable? I gave you the money for the bill."

She rolled her eyes. "I only got the shit on 'cuz you wanted it. But you are hardly here now, so I got it turned off."

He tossed the remote back onto the bed. "That was stupid. What about your kids?"

She didn't even respond to him. Both of her kids were on punishment. They didn't have a TV in their room to watch anyway.

Derrick focused on what he was doing. The sooner he got done, the faster he could get out of there. She was on some other shit. When she got up and began to move shit around, making as much noise as she could, he smiled, shook his head, and tried to ignore her.

"Are you fucking some other bitch?"

He didn't even bother to stop bagging up the hard he had cooked up earlier. "What the fuck you talking 'bout?"

"Nigga, don't play stupid." She wasn't able to yell, because her son was in the bedroom next door to hers and he could easily hear her through the walls. "You ain't been fucking me, D, so I know you fuckin' some other bitch. Who is she?"

Although she didn't know he was fucking around with Denean, hearing "bitch" upset him. She had shit twisted badly. "Who I'm fuckin ain't got shit to do with you."

She could do nothing but stare at him when he said what he said. Since he came at her that first day asking for her help, she'd been in his corner. After they started fucking, she cut off every other nigga—the ones she was fucking prior to him and the new ones trying to holla. Now this. From that moment on, she'd do her.

Before leaving, he broke her off a nice piece of crack. She took it, but she wasn't satisfied. He was playing with her emotions, and that was one thing she'd never allow.

That day when he put the crack he didn't need in the safe, Michelle paid attention. She got it. The first number to the combination. He had no idea about a woman scorned and the lengths she'd go to for paybacks.

After dropping off his last PK (package), he picked up Denean and her girl Mutter. He took Mutter to her house in Homewood before driving back to Highland Park. He parked, and he and Denean got out and went and sat in the grass. The news that she was pregnant came as a complete shock to him. He was even more fucked up that she thought he wouldn't be happy about it. "We can handle this," he told her. He had practically raised his two sisters—made their bottles, changed their diapers, and cared for them. He was happy as hell to be having a baby. "I love you, gorgeous."

Tears fell from her eyes as she hugged the father to her unborn child. Beside him, she could face anything—even her parents, whom they were going to tell together.

Immediately upon hearing the news that she was pregnant, her mother began to wail as though she had gotten the news that her only child was dead. Denean looked on in utter shock. Her mom's reaction caught her completely by surprise. Her father, whom she feared wouldn't take the news well, sat with a blank expression on his face. Torn between her mom's outburst and her dad's non-reaction, her eyes went from one to the other. She wanted to get up and comfort her mother, but she doubted if her legs were strong enough to hold her up. At that point, her father spoke.

"How many months are you?"

Her tormented eyes rested on her mother. Why wasn't he trying to comfort her? He was seated right next to her. Seeing that he wasn't, she turned her eyes to him. She loved both of her parents, and the last thing she wanted to do was hurt them. "I guess going on two months."

"Vivian," he said to his wife as he got to his feet. The look he gave his wife had its desired effect. She calmed down although she was still crying. "Good. Good. It's still early. We'll set up a doctor's appointment immediately."

Denean regained her strength at her father's words. She wanted to get up and hug him. For once, he was being the reasonable man.

"As early as tomorrow," he added. "It's' a very simple procedure and this nightmare will be over."

The meaning of his words hit Denean and Derrick at the same time. "She ain't getting no abortion," Derrick told her father.

For the first time since receiving the news that his daughter was pregnant, Troy Austin looked at the boy that had defiled his daughter and brought this disgrace to their family. He was barely able to contain the rage and contempt he felt toward him. He removed his glasses and pointed them at Derrick with a shaking hand, as though he had a weapon in his hand. "You don't have nothing to do with this!" he screamed.

"I'm the father!"

"There isn't a baby! There isn't going to be a baby. My fourteen-year-old-daughter is not going to be a mother. That's final. We'll schedule an abortion."

Tears now came to Denean's eyes. There was no way she was getting an abortion. "I thought you were against abortion." On the front door, on a front window, on both of their car rear bumpers, and on their key chains were "Say No to Abortion" slogans.

"My political beliefs, religious beliefs, and moral stance on abortion has nothing to do with anything. You are a child unable to take care of yourself. How do you expect to raise a child? No daughter of mine at fourteen is bringing a child into this world. That's final!"

She'd gone against her parents only once in her life, in the matter of their rule that she not have a boyfriend prior to sixteen. She'd be going against them again. Even if Derrick hadn't been happy about it, she still would have made the same decision she was now. "I'm not killing my baby."

If her Father had been a lighter complexion, you would have been able to see him turn beet red at her words. He was that upset. "You will get an abortion!" He advanced a few steps toward his daughter.

Derrick stood up and put himself between Denean and her father. He was her father, but not only was she Derrick's woman, but she was also the mother to his unborn child. He stood almost as tall as Denean's dad, with her father being slightly heavier by a few pounds. There was no way Derrick was going to stand by and allow anyone, including one or both of her parents, to put their hands on her.

Troy stopped short when the kid he had once welcomed into his house got to his feet to stand in front of his daughter.

"Derrick, no," Denean said as she grabbed ahold of his arm.

Troy wanted to hit the boy so bad, but had to remind himself that he was nothing but a kid. However, he couldn't allow this to happen. What his daughter failed to understand was this went far beyond his belief that abortion was immoral. This went to the core of who he was and how far he'd come. A poor boy who came up in a project up Saint Clair Village, who struggled mightily to get to where he was now. A man that brought in a six-figure income. His neighbors, most of whom were white, would get a good laugh at the niggers. That's what he feared the most. "You are throwing your life away if you decide to have this child. Do you think this street thug is going to be there for you? Ha! Until you come to your senses, and it better be quickly, you are no longer welcome in this home. If this bastard child is born, you are dead to me. When he dumps you, don't come back crying to me and your mother. Dead to me."

Denean knew her devoted Christian parents would not be happy with her pregnancy, but this was the last thing she thought would happen. She looked at her mom hoping she'd try to talk some sense into her father, but her mother turned away from her.

Unable to contain himself any longer, Derrick blurted out, "I'll take care of them both. Fuck you, nigga!" He shook Denean's hand off his arm because he wanted her dad to say one thing. To sneeze. That's all it would take.

"Babe, come on." She was on her feet now. "I'm going to have our baby. You are both upset right now, so I'll leave." She pulled Derrick toward the front door. When she turned around at the door to tell them how sorry she was, her father was coming toward her. She thought he had changed his mind.

"The key," he said, extending his hand.

Wordlessly, she removed the key from her keychain and handed it to him. She then left out.

Derrick and Denean pulled away from her house just as she broke down and the tears began to come in torrents. The last thing he wanted to do was allow her parents to see her break down. He pulled over when he was a sufficient distance away and took her into his arms. "It's going to be okay, gorgeous. I promise you that. We're going to be fine."

With all her being, she believed him, but they were only fourteen. On top of that, where was she supposed to go? Her cousin would let her live with her. Mutter would. But she was hurting. "What are we going to do? Where am I going to stay?"

He wiped away her tears. "At my house."

"And if your mom says no?"

He doubted his mom would say no, but if she did, they'd be cool. "If my mom says no, we'll get our own shit." He had more than enough money for it.

~ ~ ~

Back at her home, Troy removed everything he owned that said, "Say No to Abortion" and tossed it into the trash. She'd come around, he continued to tell himself. His daughter was reasonable.

Vivian watched her husband move about the house. She hoped they'd made the right decision. She began to pray.

~ ~ ~

Maybe the fact that she had Derrick at a young age made her more accepting of her son and Denean's predicament. Oh, she wasn't happy about it, and she made that abundantly clear. But the last thing she was going to do was turn her back on them. Her own parents—well, her mom—had kicked her out when she got pregnant with Derrick. "She's welcome to stay here."

Grateful, Denean hugged her. "Thank you!"

"Don't thank me yet, Denean. This thing that you call life just got a lot harder," she told her. One thing Denean had going for her was that the one who got her pregnant was willing to accept responsibility for the baby. Neither Derrick's dad nor her daughters' fathers had anything to do with their kids. Later Jocelyn would go talk to Denean's parents. She too would give them time to cool off.

EIGHT

When Michelle heard the news that Derrick had some little young bitch pregnant, she was hot. That he was happy about it made it that much worse. She could have given him a baby if he wanted one so bad. Thinking that her drug use was the reason they were no longer as close as they once were, she cut back on getting high and even considered entering a rehabilitation facility in the hopes that would regain his attention. She realized their relationship, if you could call it that, was illegal, but she couldn't help the way she felt. An attempt to make him jealous by having company when he came over hadn't brought about the desired effect. He told Steve, the nigga she tried to make Derrick jealous over, that he had made love for her, so he better treat her right. She wanted him to go off, to slap her around a little and tell her she better not give his pussy away to no nigga, to let her know she was still his bitch. If he did that, she'd accept him having a woman and a baby on the side. He did none of that. He simply told her he'd be back later.

He still kept his work in her bedroom, but with a baby and a bitch, how long would that last? That's what she feared.

Kelly took joy in telling her nasty-ass mom that Derrick not only had a woman, but that he had a baby on the way. Served her ass right. She knew Derrick had once been her boyfriend. Who did that? Fucked their child's boyfriend? She intended on paying her mom back in some type of way. When her mom's new boyfriend started coming around, Kelly took every available opportunity to flirt with him. She'd get out of the tub with just a towel on and just so happen to be coming out of the bathroom, just as he came out her mom's room. She'd brush up against him so he would rub against her ass. Like mother like daughter, Kelly, at only fifteen, had a bangin' body like her mom. He would try not to look, but Kelly wasn't going to be ignored.

One night while her mom slept in her room, Kelly heard Steve go into the bathroom. It was just the chance she'd been waiting on. She took off everything but her bra and panties and waited on him.

"Can you lotion my back?" she asked.

Steve took a look at her fat ass, and before he knew it, he had not only lotioned her back, but had also buried his face between his woman's daughter's legs.

Not yet ready to go all the way, Kelly allowed him to lick her to orgasm. She had gotten some of her payback, but she was nowhere near satisfied. She'd get her paybacks on her mom some more, but the biggest payback would be against Derrick. He had to pay too. Maybe she'd leak that her mother and Derrick had been fucking and make sure Denean heard. That would be good. A start anyway.

~ ~ ~

"Mutter, Mutter!" Denean's girl's mom screamed out from her chair in the living room, to no avail. "She's upstairs in her room. The little bitch has her TV blasted."

Denean smiled. She liked her girl's mom. She was funny as hell. Walking past her and up the steps, the music from her girl's room got louder. She didn't bother knocking, just opened her girl's bedroom door and yelled, "Mutta-butt!"

Mutter, seated at her vanity table, jumped as her nickname was yelled, scaring the hell out of her. She turned down the TV and stopped singing. "Bitch, I told you to stop calling me that. I ain't no damn kid no more." She hated "Mutta-butt." She was almost sixteen and was simply "Mutter."

"Told you to be ready an hour ago. Your ass still ain't dressed."

Mutter fidgeted with her hair, looking at it in the mirror at different angles. "If you would have come an hour ago, I would have been ready, but as usual, you're late. Didn't like what I had on, so I changed." Scattered on her bed were several different outfits.

She sat in her bra and panties.

Denean moved some clothes out of the way so she could sit down. The short walk up the steps had her winded. "'Bout to leave your ass."

"There," she said as she got up, finally satisfied with the way her hair was. The denim Baby Phat jean set was quickly put on. It was the latest edition (of course). She didn't have a serious baller like her girl, but the nigga she claimed kept her in the latest gear, her hair and nails done, and spending money in her purse.

The two friends complimented each other. Neither wore make-up. Just lip gloss on their lips. Where Denean was thick at five foot two, Mutter was considered slim at five foot seven and weighing 123 pounds. Her hair wasn't as long as her girl's, but she kept it done. In the looks department, neither was average. Even with her girls rocking some gray sweats and her long hair pulled back in a ponytail, she was still a dime piece. She cut off the TV. "Let's go, fat ass."

Denean got to her feet and looked at the full-length mirror on the closet door. She'd noticed her face getting fatter and her titties bigger, but she turned, pulled her sweats tight against her ass and looked over her shoulder at her butt. "Am I getting fat for real?"

Mutter wanted to say something smart, but she could see her girl was tripping about her comment. "You're pregnant, bitch. What the fuck you think was gonna happen? You got my godson growing inside of you."

Her girl was right. She just hoped once she had her son, her body would return to the way it was. And Lord, she hoped she didn't get a lot of visible stretch marks.

"Come in here rushing me 'cuz D's ass is rushing you."

"He's out running around."

Mutter stopped at the bottom of the steps and turned to look at her friend. "He better have let you use the whip, 'cuz I ain't about to jump on no bus."

Denean pushed past her and walked to the front door. "I ain't no bus chick. He bought me a truck." She opened the door.

Mutter couldn't believe it and rushed past her girl and screamed at the sight of the baby-blue Lexus SUV sitting on twenty-four inch chromed wheels. Shawna, Mutter's mom, even got up to take a look. "That's yours?"

Denean raised the remote lock and starter and hit the button, unlocking the doors. A second later the car started.

Mutter raced off her porch and flung the passenger door open. She cranked up the sounds to the $4,700 system he had installed. "Damn, bitch."

Denean smiled. She had been shocked when Derrick put $7,500 in her hand and told her to go shopping for their son, right after they got back home from finding out they were having a boy. She asked him if he was going to take her. That's when he held up the keys. Seeing the Lexus with the big ribbon on it out front almost caused her to faint. She couldn't get behind the wheel fast enough. She called Mutter and told her to be ready, but with no one home, she had to break her baby off before she left. That's why she was late getting to her girl's.

Mutter was impressed. Her girl was really shittin' on bitches now. Had her realizing that she had to step up her game. Actually, Andy, her boo, had to step his up. She didn't even know how to drive, but the nigga better teach her. If he didn't, he could wave at the wet-wet from a distance and she'd find someone else worthy of her.

As she headed around her truck, some nigga stopped his car in the middle of the street and rolled down his window.

"Damn, mami!. What's good?"

Denean opened her door and smiled. "My BD, sweety." She got in, unable to hear what he was saying because of her sounds Mutter turned up and closed the door. As she pulled out, she turned down the music some. "Bitch, is your ass death?"

As she rode by, people turned to stare. It was too cold to roll the windows down, so the people who turned to look wondered who the new baller was behind the tinted windows riding through. Life was good for Denean. Three months ago when she found out she was pregnant, she didn't think she'd ever be happy again. With the way her life had gone in the last ninety-two days, it couldn't have been any better if she had written it herself. Actually, there was one thing she'd change. Her parents..True to his words, her dad had not spoken to her since she left. She'd sent them both a text telling them they'd have a grandson soon. As with all her text messages to them over the months, they didn't respond. She missed them terribly.

Derrick had plans of his own the afternoon he sent Denean out to get shit for their son in her truck he'd bought—plans that involved pain, specifically, pain he'd feel. He wasn't a bitch, but he wasn't a freak for pain either. He now sat in the chair, not too sure he'd be able to go through with it. The decision to get a tattoo came the week before as he met his mans at the parlor to pick up some money he was owed. His boy was getting some gang shit tatted on him, but the pictures that lined the walls of the artist's work captured his attention. Motherfuckers said it didn't hurt, but Derrick wasn't really trying to hear that. A needle touching any part of your body was bound to hurt.

"You ready for this?" the artist asked just as he finished

shaving Derrick's back to make sure he had no hair there.

If this wasn't for Denean, he never would have gotten a tat. A few people cautioned him about getting the tat, but he didn't listen to them. He leaned forward and attempted to relax. "Let's do this." With one more wipe of a cloth, he then felt the needle as it bit into his flesh. He flinched. By his second hour, he wasn't really moving and he realized it didn't hurt. Just a small annoying discomfort. From start to finish, it took almost five hours.

"All done."

Derrick sat up. His legs felt funny. He'd only gotten up to stretch twice in the five hours. He wanted to get it all finished in one session. The shop was pretty full, and several people got up to take a look at his back. The artist took several pictures for his collection. It was one of his best works. Standing in front of the full-length mirror, with the artist holding a mirror in front of him so he could see his back, Derrick looked at the finished product.

On his back on the left was a baby photo of Denean's face with wings surrounding her saying an angel is born, along with 9-27-90. The picture on the right was of her as well, one that she recently took. The words "My Gorgeous Soulmate" surrounded the picture. The accuracy of the picture to tat was amazing. As soon as he saw it, he knew he'd be getting more. He actually scheduled for the following week to get something of his mom and sisters. He got the instructions on how to care for his tat, paid the man $1,200, and left out. While in the chair, he'd ignored several calls. Once in his car, he saw two were from Denean. He listened to his messages and shook his head as he listened to one of the ones he got from the woman he now had on his back for life. "Why I gotta be fucking someone 'cuz I ain't answer my phone?" he asked her when he returned her call.

"Sorry, sexy. Where you at? I wanna show you all things I got for our son."

He winced as his back came into contact with the seat. He'd have to drive leaning forward. He couldn't believe that she acted like she didn't just leave him a foul message. Lately her mood swings, as she called them, were getting crazier. "I'm on my way home from the south side." He hung up and blazed up some purple haze before pulling out. By the time he came off the Bloomfield Bridge onto Liberty Avenue, he was feeling it from the weed.

~ ~ ~

Denean was pulling out one thing after the other showing him all the clothes she bought their son. Derrick had to bring the stroller, bed, tub, rocker, and all the heavy stuff in from the truck.

"You got shit he ain't gonna be able to fit," he pointed out.

"He'll grow into it."

He didn't tell her by then a new style would probably be out.

"Why you keep making that face?" Denean asked him.

He hadn't noticed that he was making a face. He shrugged, and that aggravated the tat. He needed another blunt. He thought Mutter would be with her and he'd get her to take off the bandages that covered both tats. But Denean told him she had dropped her off in East Liberty where her nigga snatched her up.

"Denean!" came a shout from downstairs announcing the arrival of Derrick's sisters and mom back from their trip to the zoo.

Denean sighed and rolled her eyes. She knew what was coming as she heard the two girls running up the steps.

Side by side they burst into the room and went straight to

Denean, who was sitting on the bed. They pressed their heads to her stomach.

"Did he move?" Tamika asked.

"Earlier," she admitted.

"Aw, man," they said as one.

Denean pulled up her shirt and rubbed her exposed stomach. It wasn't too big, but you could tell she was pregnant.

"He be always moving when I ain't here."

"Wake up, nephew," Tamika pleaded.

From the moment they found out she was having a baby, the two had swarmed Denean—never far from their nephew, waiting for him to move. Derrick knew his sisters would keep Denean preoccupied. He went off in search of his mother, and located her sitting in the dining room smoking a Newport cigarette.

"You'd think those two weren't sisters the way they fussed and fought all day. I smoked a half a pack today at least." Trying to quit, she'd cut back to less than five a day. Today she had a minor setback.

He'd come to that conclusion himself a long time ago. He gingerly took off his shirt. "Mom, I need you to help me, right quick."

At the sight of the bandages, she almost screamed, but she noticed a part of the tattoo coming out of the bottom of the bandage. "How in the hell did you get a tattoo? Ain't you suppose to get a parent's consent if you're not eighteen?" She began to remove the bandages. At the sight of them both, she stared in awe. "They're beautiful."

"I'm getting you, Mika, and Chelle's name on me next week," he announced.

Tattoos were the in thing now. Everyone seemed to have at least one nowadays. Jocelyn had even thought about getting one before. Seeing how nice her son's were, she thought she might even go when he went back and get all her kids' names on her. "I take it you haven't showed her yet?"

He shook his head no. "'Bout to right now." He led the way back up the steps to his room, where his sisters were still trying to get their nephew to move. "Come look at my back, Mika and Chelle."

What the two wanted to do is wait for the baby to move. They got to their feet reluctantly, and Denean pulled her shirt back down, thankful for the interruption.

"That's Denean," Mika pointed out.

"That's hard." Rochelle said.

She had no idea what either girl was talking about. She wondered why Derrick no longer had on his shirt, and then he turned so she could see his back. Her eyes watered even as she got to her feet to take a closer look. The tats of her on his back meant more to her than the truck and all the other things he'd ever given her combined. Like with the tats, she wanted their love to last forever. She turned him and kissed him passionately.

With Jocelyn coughing to get her attention, she broke off the kiss. "Sorry." She tried not to show too much affection in front of his mom and sisters, out of respect. Denean grabbed up her phone. "Turn around, sexy. I want to send Mutter a picture of your tats." She took several and sent the one she liked best. "When can I get one of you on me?"

He knew she'd want one, so he asked the dude about it. "You can't get one 'cuz you pregnant."

She didn't like it, but as soon as she had their son, she was getting Derrick's face on her body somewhere.

Several things would delay her getting her tattoo in six months...

Michelle stood in her doorway long after Derrick had driven off. She watched him as he rode down the street and got out at the row he lived at. And ten minutes later, she saw him get back in his car and drive down the hill. The neighbor she'd been talking to as cover so she could keep an eye on Derrick was in mid-sentence when Michelle cut her off.

"Girl, I got to use the bathroom." She stepped in her house, locked the door, and raced up the steps to her room. She locked that door as well. She repeated all three numbers in her head the entire time, hoping that this time she didn't have it wrong. For months, she'd stolen glances over his shoulders trying to get the combination. This time she had it. Or at least she thought she did. If she didn't, she'd go back and try to steal glances as he opened the safe. She didn't know if he intentionally blocked her view, but he did. That's why it had taken her months to get three simple numbers:17-28-36.

Her hands trembled as she carefully put in each number. When she put in the last number, she closed her eyes and pulled on the door handle. To her delight, the door swung open. Twice she locked it and opened it to make sure she had it correct. Both times it swung open. He'd left her with some crack, so she had no need to dip into the zip lock bag.

Over the next few weeks though, she'd open the safe and break herself off a nice chunk. Derrick never said anything, so she thought he didn't suspect a thing. She was wrong.

~ ~ ~

With each passing day, Kelly's anger at her mom and Derrick grew. She wanted them both to pay. The rumor that she got started either didn't reach Denean's ears or it didn't matter to her. In any event, Derrick and Denean remained together. The fact he had fucked her mother wasn't really what ate at Kelly. She was fast learning most niggas would fuck anything. Since her basement experience with Derrick, her sexual experiences with boys her age and even grown men had grown. She was no longer a virgin. Steve was a favorite sex partner of hers, but not the one she really wanted. She would have probably forgotten all about her revenge if the latest incident with Derrick hadn't taken place two days prior.

Opening the door for him, Kelly took the opportunity to let him know she was ready. Without warning, she reached out and grabbed his dick through his jeans. She felt him grow in her hand. "I want you to fuck me, D, and let me suck on this dick."

He removed her hands. At one time he would have jumped at the opportunity, but he had just had to explain to Denean about some rumors she heard, including one in which he was supposedly fucking Michelle. He lied of course, but he decided he was done with the cheating shit. "I'm cool, shorty," he had said.

Everyone was trying to get in her pants. Having Derrick turn her down had her feeling some type of way. Lately she hadn't heard him fucking her mother, but that didn't mean he wasn't. He still came over and spent time up in her bedroom. She often wondered what he did during those visits. One evening while her mom was in the tub, Kelly went into her mom's room for a quick look around, and came across the safe in the closet. Word on the street was Derrick was balling. The money in the safe had to be a lot. She now had her payback. She didn't want to just take his money. She wanted to take it and somehow have Derrick think it was her Mom that did it. Somehow, some way, she'd get them both.

~ ~ ~

It wasn't the nigga Michelle wanted behind her pounding her ass, but he wasn't a bad substitute. Using Steve in an attempt to make Derrick jealous hadn't worked out. It did give her the occasional dick she required. "That's right, nigga. Fuck me in my ass!"

He grunted, pulled her by her hair, and with his mouth close to her ear said, "You like getting fucked in your ass, don't you?"

To Michelle it sometimes got her pussy wetter by getting hit in her ass. This was one of those times. She fingered herself as he continued to ram into her ass. "Yeah, oh fuck!" she screamed as she had another orgasm. "Fuck me harder, nigga. Fuck this phat ass."

Her words spurned him on, but as he felt himself getting ready to cum, he tried to stop. Michelle continued to back up hard against him, not allowing him a reprieve.

Knowing it was a lost cause, he forced himself hard into her, causing her to fall flat on her stomach. "Where you want me to cum?"

She knew he wanted her to say in her mouth. She'd gone straight from her ass to mouth before, but it felt too good to stop.

"Cum in my ass. Fill my ass with your hot cum, nigga!"

He did just that as he convulsed on top of her. He didn't pull out until his dick went soft in her ass.

Putting on her robe, she got up and went to the bathroom to wash up and get Steve a warm soapy rag so he could clean his dick off. When she stepped out of the bathroom, she looked into her daughter's room and saw her daughter sitting on her bed. That her raunchy sex was overheard didn't faze her. With no words spoken between them, she returned to her room and handed Steve the rag.

While Michelle was in the bathroom, Kelly had opened the door and given Steve the finger. She left before he could say anything. He loved fucking her young ass, but she wasn't as freaky as her mom. He loved fucking them both, and once Michelle fell asleep, he'd sneak into Kelly's room and make it up to her. At least that was his plan before he lay there and got tired.

Michelle lay beside him giving her decision one last going over. Once she did what she decided, there was no turning back. Steve told her there was a drought and that's why he couldn't look out. Originally she hooked up with him because the nigga handed over a few stones. That hadn't been the case since she hooked up with Derrick. With him being slimy, she nearly changed her mind. She listened as his breathing became lighter, indicating he was almost sleeping. "You still looking for some work?"

Hearing her words only reminded him that she was nothing but a crackhead. That's why he treated her the way he did. It's also why he preferred Kelly over her. No matter how freaky she was or sexy she could be when she dressed up, when you got right down to it, she was a crackhead. Why couldn't she just let him sleep? "Yeah, nigga is tapped."

There wasn't a motherfuckin' drought. A few feet from where she lay was a safe full of crack. The only thing tapped was the nigga's pockets. She realized awhile ago that Steve was nothing but an eight-ball hustler. He would never be on Derrick's level. That was alright; he would serve her purpose. "What you trying to snatch up?"

He was too tired to laugh. She acted like she could put him on or some shit. Her question really didn't deserve an answer, but he asked, "Why?"

"I might be able to help you."

That peeked his interest. What was truly the case was he bought a ride for $1,800, his entire stash. His lying ass baby mom was supposed to give him enough to cop a quarter, but she nixed it after she claimed he gave her gonorrhea. He denied it of course. Still he went to Oakland to the clinic and got treated. He was faced with the real possibility of having to pawn his chain. It wouldn't be the first time. And now this. He smiled to himself and rolled to face her. She got an SSI check and welfare for her kids.

He began to play with her nipple. It responded to his touch. "Help me how?"

She got up and went to her dresser and took out the ounce she'd put there earlier.

She flicked on the light.

At the sight of the hard, he sat up. This was his lucky day. He reached for the zip lock baggie.

"Nigga, how much loot you holding?" She moved the hard out of his reach. He smiled and began to feel her up. His fuck game was good, but it wasn't good enough to get a ounce of hard for free.

He couldn't come up with a response fast enough. "You want me to get rid of that for you?"

On some real shit, she could probably get rid of it on her own, but didn't want to take the chance of it getting back to Derrick. She didn't want to let the nigga think he was doing her a favor though. "You want me to get you on since your pockets are on E." He hadn't admitted that he was broke, but she now knew that he was.

He realized he didn't have much of a choice but to admit the truth, so he nodded his head yes.

She had this nigga. Saw it all in his eyes. Guess it was the same look she'd given a nigga when she was broke and looking for a lookout. Hungry. Willing to do just about anything to get what you wanted. Ever since she took her first hit, niggas had been coming at her sideways. Attempting to give her a stone for some head and/or pussy. It was downright degrading the way she had to basically beg to get a blast. The only hustler that ever treated her halfway decent was Derrick. And she was about to fuck him over.

He hadn't said anything about moving his work out, but she knew it was coming. She had to look out for herself. She had to put this bottom level wannabe hustler in his place. She put one leg up on the bed exposing her pussy. He told her he didn't eat pussy. She knew he said it because she smoked hard. Well now it was time for paybacks. "Come here and lick this pussy for marni. Show me you are on my team."

He hesitated. It's not that her pussy stank; it was that…he didn't have time to complete his thought before she put her hand behind head and pulled him forward. His face came into contact with her pussy and he started to lick.

By the time the night was over and before she gave him half an ounce, she had him not only eating her pussy, but had also made him lick her ass—a first for Steve.

"Lick this ass, nigga. Suck it like you love it."

He did just that—all the while thinking of the come up.

Sedated, Michelle lay on her back, her ass wet from the nigga's tongue, and looked at him. He was her bitch now. "You can take the lil bit of shit I just gave you and run off with the money. I ain't gonna chase you about it. Or you can get rid of it, bring me my cut, and I'll look out again. As long as you come correct, I'll look out. The choice is yours."

He sat with cum around his mouth and a tart taste on his tongue when she told him that.

From that day up until two months later, he began to get his

ROBERT TORRES

shit from her. Never more than an ounce at a time, but it was more than he was used to getting. The only problem he had is he could never just hand over the money and get more work. She always had him do some sick perverted shit. Like now as he lay back in the tub with her standing over him.

"Open your mouth, nigga. Mama got a nice shower for you."

Like an obedient dog, his mouth opened. Piss streamed down into his mouth and on his face and chest as he got his first golden shower. He accepted it all. He had a bigger plan. He had to find out where she was getting all the crack. He wanted in on a bigger level.

Kelly heard the way her mom talked to Steve. The nigga was a lame. A nickel and dime hustler. She thought of herself as a dime bitch. He wasn't worthy of her pussy, so she cut him off. She heard him some nights turning her door handle, but she made sure she locked it the nights he stayed over. Her pussy was only for niggas that could afford it. Steve wasn't one of those niggas with his hoopty and empty pockets.

She'd gotten in an argument with her mom earlier in the day, and that's why she left her bedroom door slightly open when Steve spent the night. It wasn't long before he eased into her room.

She ignored him as he told her he was sorry for whatever he'd done. He was right. He was sorry. She took the hundred he offered her and tossed it on her end table. "What the fuck you think a punk-ass hundred gonna get you?"

"Can I lick it?"

"Nigga, you can't even smell it."

He knew she wouldn't give back his money. "What can I get for it then?" He no longer had the swag he once had, before Michelle's remarks and perverse sexual acts stripped it away. Now he was truly what he'd really been from the beginning:

100

regular.

He was nothing to her. As she looked at him standing there begging, a plan came to her—one in which she could use this lame. "All you get is to lick and suck on my toes." She lifted her right leg and raised it to his lips.

She had the game fucked up. For a Franklin, all he got was to lick her toes. As she began to lower her leg, he grabbed her calf. It wasn't worse than the shit her mom had him doing, and better than nothing at all. He slowly began to lick and suck on her foot.

The shit was starting to feel good to her. She kicked off her covers and began to finger herself. She had him and he'd do what she wanted him to do. Fucking him now would be so she could get her shit off. She was horny.

When her door came crashing open, Steve jumped to his feet. As he sucked on her feet, he'd taken out his dick and was stroking it. Now he fumbled with it as he tried to put it away.

"Bitch nigga, my daughter!" Michelle screamed as she punched him and scratched at his face.

He covered up and raced down the steps and out of the house, with Michelle on his heels.

Outside, she searched for a rock or brick so she could shatter his window. He drove off before she found one. She returned to her house intent on killing her nasty-ass daughter, and found her still sitting in her bed in her bra and panties.

Serves her ass right, she thought. Seeing her mom's intent, she jumped up, refusing to take an ass kicking without fighting back.

The two stared at each other. Michelle could see the change in her nearly sixteen-year-old. She was ready to bang. It wasn't that she was afraid. She was just caught off guard. "Nasty bitch, how long has it been going on?"

"Not as long as you and Derrick. And if I'm a nasty bitch,

I got it from my nasty-ass momma."

It was then that she realized her child hated her. Michelle left without saying anything and went into her room.

Kelly wanted her crackhead-ass mom to act like she wanted to get at her. She hated her. Recently one of the niggas she was fucking bought her a minute phone. She called Steve's cell as she stepped into her pants. He picked up. "Where are you?"

He had driven away as fast as he could, trying to get away from Michelle. He had really fucked up big time. He had to pull over because he was shaking too bad to drive. Just when he decided he'd go get a drink from the Horoscope Bar on Penn Avenue, his phone rang. He saw it was a number Kelly had called him from before. He almost didn't answer it. "Yeah."

"Where the fuck you at?"

All he could think of was going to prison for fucking a young bitch. Michelle was probably talking to the police right now. "You got to tell 'em we ain't never did shit, yo."

"Stop bitchin, nigga. Come get me."

She was straight tripping now. There was no way he was ever going anywhere near her again. "Naw, shorty, it's over."

"Ain't shit over, nigga. Get the fuck up here and pick me up or I'll call the cops and tell them you raped me. I'll be walking down Atlantic. You got ten minutes," she told him, and hung up on him. She finished getting dressed and left, not bothering to tell her mom she was leaving. Having to tell that bitch anything was over.

Steve was noided as hell. He didn't know if Kelly was setting him up and the jakes was lying in wait for him. He came up Aiken, the opposite hill she told him to, so he could see if there were any cops in front of her house. There weren't. Driving past the house, it didn't look like anything was up. He drove down Atlantic and saw Kelly walking. He pulled up beside her and she quickly got in. "Where is your mom?"

She ignored his question. "Fuck her. You tryin' to be put on to this lick?"

"What you talkin' 'bout?" He turned his radio down even lower.

"There's a safe in my mom's closet with a lot of money in it."

He understood now. Some nigga obviously had to be looking out for her and she let him stash his shit in her spot. What he couldn't figure is what nigga would be stupid enough to trust a crackhead. "Whose safe is it?"

She didn't see why that was important, but she told him. "Young D from the Wall."

"Derrick?"

She nodded yes.

He wasn't too surprised for two reasons. Word on the street was the nigga had some change, and only a fool or a young nigga would trust a crackhead. He couldn't figure out why he kept his shit at Michelle's. Kelly gave him the answer to his last question.

"Yeah, that nigga. He's been fucking my mom for a minute."

He laughed more out of relief than anything. Here this bitch was trippin', and she was fucking a young nigga. He saw Kelly was mad and he remembered. "Didn't you used to fuck with the nigga?"

"Is you in on this lick or do I got to get somebody else?"

"Naw, I'm in."

"Good, you got to get two or three more niggas." She began to tell him her plan—one that would have her mom being blamed. Her revenge would be complete.

As he listened to her detail the plan, Steve tweaked it a little in his head. He didn't have to tell her that just yet.

103

~ ~ ~

As Michelle's eyes flicked open and she realized this wasn't a nightmare, she immediately pissed on herself. She'd gone to sleep early, only to be awakened by a masked person pressing a gun hard into her forehead. She had this nightmare plenty of times, but this time it was real.

"Sit up, you pissy bitch," the masked man ordered. "If you scream or yell, I'ma let loose right in your muttafuckin' face."

Pissing on herself was an involuntary reaction. She told herself to remain calm and she'd get out of this. Her calmness left when she saw two more masked men, one of whom had her scantily clad daughter, in just her bra and panties, by her arm. That's also when she saw the chain dangling on the neck of the one that held her daughter. "Steve."

He forgot to tuck the chain. He really didn't give a fuck. He removed his mask. "Yeah, bitch, it's me. Now open the safe."

She lost her cool as she realized this bitch-ass nigga, whom she hadn't seen since the night she chased him out of her shit, had dared to come up in her home. Once she told Derrick, his ass would be dealt with. She didn't get the chance to tell him she wasn't opening shit, because the one holding the gun on her smacked her with the barrel on the side of her head. She fell back on the bed, dazed.

It was Kelly who screamed as she watched the light-skinned nigga slap her mom, opening up a large gash on her head. She broke away from Steve's loose grip on her arm and charged the nigga. This wasn't how it was supposed to go. All she told them to do when she let them in her back door a few minutes ago was to scare her mom into opening the safe. They weren't supposed to harm her. Now blood streamed down her mom's face.

For her bravery, light skin rewarded her with a vicious slap to her head, dazing her and sending her crashing to the floor.

Dazed herself but ignoring the pain and blood, Michelle reached down for her daughter. "Open the safe now, bitch!"

She had no idea what they'd do to her and her daughter if she refused. She knew Steve wasn't the leader of this three-man crew. Her son stayed over at a friend's house this night and she was glad. All she had to do was get herself and her daughter out of this.

She'd explain to Derrick how she opened the safe when she wasn't even supposed to have the combination. He'd be mad, but at least they'd be alive.

Kelly managed to sit up. Her mouth was busted and bleeding from the backhanded slap. So her mom didn't recognize Steve, Kelly had told the light-skinned nigga to do all the talking. Her eyes sought out Steve's. "This isn't the way it's supposed to go."

Steve's plan had him getting out on Kelly once he got the money, but he didn't want anyone to get hurt. "Ease up, dawg."

"If this bitch don't open the safe in thirty seconds, I'm putting one in her daughter's head," light skin threatened. High off the three X-pills he'd taken, he grabbed Kelly off the floor by her hair and jammed his gun to her head.

Her daughter's words didn't escape her. That she set this robbery up meant little to Michelle. She'd deal with her later. "I'll open it. Please don't hurt my baby."

Tears fell from Kelly's eyes as she heard her mom. "Mommy," she said in a voice laced with fear.

Years had passed since her child had called her mommy. She loved her baby. When all of this was over, they'd have to talk, they'd regain the closeness they once shared.

Michelle smiled at her daughter. "It's okay, baby. I'll open it." She got up, went to the safe, and got down and opened its before getting up and taking her daughter into her arms.

Light skin pulled the contents of the safe out.

Seeing the hard and powder was slightly disappointing to Steve. Now he knew where she was getting the shit to give him. Also, there wasn't as much cash as he thought would be in the safe, but from the large quantity of both the hard and soft, he knew he'd be straight after he sold it all.

On the bed, Michelle continued to comfort her daughter. "You got what you came for, now go." She knew once Derrick found out niggas stole his shit, he'd deal with them.

"Let's bounce, niggas," the third member of their squad, named Kush, said.

Light skin held the three zip lock baggies in his left hand. He held enough work to change his whole life. It was also enough for the nigga who lost it to want it back. He had to think. All it took was one of these bitches telling Derrick who had his shit. He'd come for him. He wasn't about to look over his shoulder every day. "Niggas, these bitches got to go."

Both Steve and Kush weren't down with that. They'd come to rob someone, not catch a double homicide. That was life. Maybe even the death penalty if they were caught. Neither got to tell light skin they didn't have to kill them, before two gunshots caused them both to jump.

The slug Michelle took in the chest propelled her body back into the headboard. Her child fell off the bed. The pain was so intense Michelle couldn't even yell. "Oh God."

Steve raised his gun and shot light skin in the face, killing him instantly out of fear. He was on some other shit, and by the look in his eyes, Steve feared light skin intended on killing him next.

Kush had seen enough. None of this shit was worth it. He turned to run, but a bullet from Steve's gun entered his back.

Knowing that all the gunshots woke the neighbors and someone probably called the cops, he quickly grabbed up the drugs and ran out the back door, jumped a fence, and ran down a hillside to Columbo Street, where he had parked his car.

Rolling across the bed, Michelle got down next to her daughter. Kelly lay on her back, her eyes wide with fear, blood oozing out of her mouth.

"I'm sorry, Mommy."

"Shhhhh. Don't try to talk." She dialed 911 and gave them her address.

"I love you and I'm sorry," Kelly managed to get out with her last breath.

She couldn't believe her daughter was dead. Not knowing if she was going to live, she used her last little bit of strength to dial Derrick's number. "Steve did it. Steve," she said and lost consciousness.

He almost didn't answer the call. "Hello." What he heard made him sit up, causing Denean to awaken.

"What's wrong?"

He tried to ask her what she was talking about, but got no response. Steve did what? he asked himself as he got up and quickly put on some clothes.

"D, what's wrong?"

"I don't know. That was Michelle. I got to run up the street real quick." He left out in a hurry. As soon as he got to the end of the row, he saw a lone cop car and two cops positioned behind their car. They had a light shining on Michelle's house.

"This is the police. Occupants of 5310, put down your weapons and come out with your hands up," one cop using a bullhorn ordered.

More cop cars came, along with a TV news crew. The street was blocked off and cops evacuated neighbors from their homes. A swat team arrived, and after giving their last warning, barged into the house.

Denean was now standing next to Derrick. Everyone in the

neighborhood seemed to be awake and outside now and they all stood behind the police barricade waiting to find out what was going on. Derrick saw the paramedics bring Michelle out. When three medical examiner vans pulled up, everyone began to wonder who was killed.

There weren't many answers that night. He wouldn't find out Kelly and two others died until nine o'clock in the morning. He didn't know how it happened, but he did know who did it. And the nigga was living on borrowed time.

T EN

Several things prevented Derrick from going after Steve immediately. The nigga disappeared, he had no idea where he lived, and he had to wait several days to talk to Michelle. The gunshot she suffered went in and out of her torso hitting no vital organs. After finding out Kelly was one of the ones killed, Derrick blamed himself. If he hadn't kept his shit in their crib, none of this shit would have happened. Michelle hadn't told him of Kelly's involvement. She did confess to sneaking peeks over his shoulder to get the combination to the safe and taking a couple ounces over the months. He wasn't slow. He realized Michelle was dipping into his shit a long time ago, but she wasn't hurting him, so he acted like he didn't notice.

Denean hadn't been close friends with Kelly, but she knew her. What shocked her more than Kelly's death was how people responded to it. Many deemed it life in the hood. Denean wasn't from the hood, but even if she was, she wouldn't have accepted it simply as life in the hood. On her hands, she counted seven people that she knew personally that had been killed in her fourteen plus years of living.

In school, people said things like, "Shit happens," "It goes down in the hood," etc. Hearing it all not only saddened her, but terrified her. Her son would soon be born, living in the same hood where shit goes down, where a fifteen-year-old is gunned down in her home. No, that's not the life she wanted for herself or her child. The only good thing she got out of this incident was a call from her parents. After watching the news coverage of the shooting, they called her to make sure she was okay. She was on her way to their home when she tried to call

Derrick for the fifth time. He still didn't pick up, and she began to worry.

Michelle confirmed that it was Steve, the nigga she'd been fucking with, that was responsible for taking Derrick's shit and killing Kelly. She had no idea where he lived. Derrick tried not to make it too obvious, but he asked around and found out that Steve lived out Tarentum. He didn't know too much about Tarentum, but he knew it wasn't that big.

He'd find him. He headed there with only one thing on his mind: killing Steve's bitch ass.

Steve was going on nervous energy. To keep it a hundred, he was scared to death. He knew the system well enough to know that although he had only killed two people, he'd be charged with all four murders if caught. He considered running to family down in South Carolina, but knew he couldn't do it in the condition he was in. Just making it to his house in Tarentum was difficult. He stayed in his apartment for two straight days, jumping at every loud noise, thinking it was the police breaking down the door. He wasn't able to relax much and when he drifted off in a fitful sleep, the killings replayed in his dreams. He usually woke up in a deep sweat, and at 6:15 p.m. the third day after the killings, was no different. He was caught, found guilty, and sentenced to life in this dream.

He didnt want anyone to die. This was just supposed to be a quick lick. If it wasn't for crazy-ass light skin, it never would have happened.

That he killed light skin didn't bother him. It was the other three dying that ate at his conscience. Shit happened, he tried to convince himself, but that didn't make him feel any better.

The drugs sat under his bed untouched. Once shit died down, he'd unload it all. A dead man told no tales. That saying kept going through his head. There was no one to lead the police back to him. On the Highland Park Bridge the night of the killings, he tossed his gun into the river. By the third day, he thought he was going to get away with it. The last thing he'd do was tell someone what took place in Michelle's house that night.

~ ~ ~

Tarentum, Derrick found out, was smaller than he thought. He got off Route 28 at the Tarentum/New Kensington exit around 5:00 p.m. It took him no time to locate someone who knew Steve.

"That nigga lives up on 9th," the white girl pushing a stroller with a half/half baby in it said. "You wouldn't happen to be selling any weed?"

"Naw." He drove off, passing a sign that had 3rd Street on it. He was only six blocks from where the nigga laid his head. He tried to control the rage that was building in him. Over the past days, he thought of nothing but killing the nigga. Steve was as good as dead.

As he drove down 9th Street, he saw Steve's ride parked in front of a building. From the looks of it, there were only six to eight apartments in the building. He had no idea which one the nigga lived in. He wasn't going to go door to door. Besides, if Steve saw him, he wouldn't open the door, and he might let his guns do the talking first. Derrick wasn't willing to take a chance. Going to the end of the street, he parked and got out. A bench was near and it still enabled him to see the front of the building and Steve's car. He took out his phone and saw all the missed calls. He called Denean back first. "Hey, gorgeous."

"Why was your phone going straight to voicemail?"

"Handling something and didn't notice it was off."

"That's bullshit. Are you with some bitch?"

He knew that was coming. "You hit me up all those times

111

to bitch?"

"I called you 'cuz I was worried," she cried out before she hung up.

He pushed Send, calling her right back.

"What?"

"My bad, sexy. I'm out handling something."

She blew her nose and tried to stifle her tears. "All I ask is to keep your phone on. The police came by wanting to talk to you."

He wanted to hear more, but just then he saw Steve come out and get in his car. "Sexy, I got to go. I'll call you right back." He hung up and ran the short distance to his car. He had no idea where the nigga was headed, but his life was corning to an end.

~ ~ ~

Enough time had gone by that if the jakes were looking for Steve, they would have kicked his door in by now. Hungry, he decided to run out and get a hoagie.

The pizza shop was only a few blocks away, really walking distance, but he didn't want to be out in the open like that. It was beginning to turn dark when he jumped in his ride and pulled out. He didn't pay attention to the car at the end of the block as its lights came on and began to follow him.

The only thing that stopped Derrick from driving right up next to the nigga and emptying his entire clip into him was Steve had no bag in his hand and he was dressed in a black tee and a pair of black Dickies. Derrick didn't think he'd leave all the work in the car, so it meant it had to be in his crib. He still didn't know which apartment was his, so even if he did have enough time to jump out after he killed him and get the keys, he'd have to try every door and then locate his stash. He decided he had to catch Steve slippin'.

Steve passed a police cruiser on his way to the pizza shop. It noided the hell out of him. He considered going back to his crib, but the lone cop didn't even look his way as they passed each other. Stop! he told himself. There was no way they could be on him. Everyone was dead, or so he thought. If he would have watched the news once in the last three days, he would have known that Michelle had survived. And also that the Zone 5 Police station and the city chief of police were working in conjunction with another county to bring in a person of interest. Those two facts might have convinced him to head to South Carolina immediately. He hadn't bothered with the news though.

He did catch talk on the Steelers tough road to the Super Bowl. All their playoff games would be on the road. If they made it, it would be the first time in NFL history a team traveled on the road and reached the Super Bowl. A devoted Steelers fan, Steve thought they'd do it. He parked and got out. He was on cloud nine.

Derrick watched him walk into the shop, but didn't see him come out.

As he waited for his steak hoagie, Steve went over everything in his head. Maybe it all turned out for the best. He had no intention of giving Kelly anything after the lick anyway. Of course, she would have been heated and would have run her mouth and then Derrick might... Yeah, he decided it was for the best. Once he got to the crib, he'd call Alisha—a white girl—and have her swing through. He had to go back to normal. He was hungry and horny.

After he got his sandwich and left the pizza shop, he got in his car and started up his car, prepared to take a quick bite of his hoagie. He took a look in his rearview mirror making sure no car was coming, and then he saw Derrick, causing the hoagie to fall to the floor.

"Pull out, nigga," Derrick instructed. He didn't want someone to come out of the shop and see what was going on.

The gun was pressed firmly just behind his right ear. As Steve saw Derrick raise up from hiding in the back, he almost pissed on himself. He had no idea how Derrick knew he had his shit, but he obviously did. "Please don't kill me," he begged as he pulled away from the curb. His eyes searched for a cop, hoping that he came across one so he could do something to get his attention.

Derrick wanted to put a bullet in the nigga's head so bad—to empty his clip in it. "All I want is my shit."

There was no sense in acting stupid. Derrick obviously knew something. Why else would he come way out to Tarentum and put a gun to his head, if he didn't know he had it? Steve saw the look in the young niggas eyes. He would shoot if provoked. Steve wouldn't do shit to make him mad. "Your shit at my crib, D. It's all there too."

"Take me there."

Steve drove two blocks in silence. "I didn't kill Michelle and Kelly. The nigga light skin killed them." He looked in the mirror to see how Derrick was taking the news. He had to get him on his side. "I was chilling with Michelle when light skin and another nigga barged in. I didn't even know there was a safe in the closet. They made her open it, and then light skin shot and killed them both. I had my strap under the pillows. I killed them both. I saw the work and snatched it up. I didn't know it was yours."

Derrick knew most of what Steve said was a lie. On some real shit, the nigga was dead regardless. When Derrick had ridden by the apartment building earlier, he saw a rear parking lot. "Park in the back and hand me the keys," he instructed. "You got a strap on you? Tell me now, 'cuz if I find out you lying, I'll kill you."

Once they parked, Derrick got out of the back, making sure he kept his eye on Steve, and then had Steve get out. He gave him a fast pat down. "You can try to run or yell out. You might get a few steps away or a couple words out, but you'll die soon after. You feel me?"

"I ain't gonna try nothing." Steve just wanted to live. Once he got out of this, he was going straight. No more drug selling or nothing. He might even find a woman and have a kid—a son. Maybe even a daughter. He just didn't want to die.

They encountered no one as they made it to Steve's apartment on the second level. By the time Derrick handed him back his keys, his hands were shaking so bad it took him several times to open the door. They both stepped in. As soon as Derrick locked the door, Steve thought once again about how bad he wanted to live. He began to cry.

"Lay flat on your stomach, your arms outstretched, and don't move. Where is my shit?"

Snot ran down Steve's nose as he sobbed. He did as he was told. "It's under the bed in the bag. It's all there."

Derrick had no sympathy for the nigga. He pulled the bag out and saw his three bags of work. It looked like it was all there. He put the strap across his body and zipped it. He stood over Steve looking down at the back of his head.

Steve was crying harder. He knew Derrick was standing over him. "Please don't kill me. Please man," he begged. He reached out and grabbed at Derrick's leg.

"If shit would have jumped off the way you described it, you might have had a chance to live."

"I swear."

"Michelle ain't die, nigga."

Piss and shit escaped Steve's bowels just as the bullet entered the back of his head.

115

Brain matter and blood splattered all over—some of it getting on Derrick's pant legs and shoes. For good measure, Derrick put two more into Steve's head. The noise from the gun was loud inside the apartment. Derrick exited fast because he knew someone was calling the police right now. He made sure he hadn't touched shit in Steve's car or apartment. He had to walk the blocks back to the pizza shop where he had parked his car. As he walked slowly, several police cars zoomed past him headed toward Steve's apartment. Headed back to Pittsburgh on 28, Derrick put his shit on cruise control at fifty-seven.

The chief of police of Tarentum got the call at his home from the chief of Pittsburg concerning one of his residents in connection with the triple murder in Pittsburgh at 8:10 p.m. Wanting to be in on the bust, he gathered himself, kissed his wife, and called the local news station. He wanted to be in the coverage of the big arrest.

Might help his re-election bid as chief.

After getting everyone situated, they used a battering ram and took down the door. What they discovered was the dead, but still warm body of the reported suspect. He called the chief s direct number in Pittsburgh. "Dan, I got some bad news. Just got here at the suspect's house. He's suffered several gunshot wounds to the back of the head."

This latest killing stopped the investigation of the triple homicide in Garfield, but it opened a new one. A killer was still on the loose.

ELEVEN

No remorse, nightmares, or adverse effects happened to Derrick in the following days after he killed Steve. A homicide detective did want to talk to him after a check of the last call Michelle made—his number had showed up. Derrick explained he had no idea why Michelle had called him, that he hadn't talked to her at all that night. The detective also asked Derrick about the safe in her closet. On that too he had no idea what the detective was talking about. No, he wouldn't leave the city. "I'm only fourteen," he told the baffled detective.

Derrick visited Michelle at the hospital. He didn't have to tell her Steve was handled. He knew she knew it was him that killed Steve. She was in no danger of dying, but the death of her daughter had taken a lot out of her. Parents shouldn't ever have to bury their child—especially one only fifteen years old. Michelle hadn't prepared for this day. She had no insurance on her child, nor had she saved up any money to bury her daughter. Derrick told her not to worry about anything. "I'll get someone on her funeral arrangements. You just focus on getting better."

"I can't believe she is dead."

Derrick had a hard time believing that as well. He got up and hugged her gently, both of them crying.

She tried to apologize again for stealing from him.

That shit didn't bother him. Neither would be the same again.

~ ~ ~

By the time of Kelly's funeral, Michelle was out of the hospital. Her son was taken from her by CYS and placed in foster care. He attended his sister's funeral as well.

The day they put Kelly in the ground, Derrick lay next to Denean rubbing her stomach absentmindedly.

Kelly's death affected Denean as well. She attended school with the girl—middle and high school. She knew Derrick had messed with her once. She held no resentment over that. The whole situation was sad. And more than that, it gave her a reason to pause, reflect, and think. Pretty soon she'd be responsible for another life. Their son was due in July. What world would he be coming into? A world where reaching the age of twenty-five was considered an accomplishment—a world of death. Simply life in the hood? Hell no!

Not for her child and not for her or the man she loved. She pressed her hand over his and said, "I want to move."

They'd just finished making love, and he was already nodding off when she spoke.

He heard her, but wasn't sure. "Huh?"

She didn't bother repeating herself. He heard her. Soon she heard his light snoring. She knew how much he loved his hood. Garfield was the only place he had ever lived. What she wondered was if he loved it more than her and their son. That's the decision he would soon be forced to make. Her mind was made up.

Kelly's death wasn't only affecting Denean. Jocelyn sat at her dining room table thinking while drinking a cup of coffee and smoking a cigarette. Her thoughts were on the place she called home: Garfield. She was a three-generation Garfellin. Her grandma and mother both grew up and lived in the community—in the same projects on Cornwall Street. Cornwall was all she knew, "Da Wall," as it was affectionately known to those living on its street. There were people there who had lived up on its hill for forty plus years.

Parents died and the kids took over the project home as though it was passed down in a will. There were grown men and women, some with kids of their own, still living with their parent(s) in a basement or the room they had their entire lives. For Jocelyn, it held both good and bad memories. Most of her firsts had taken place on its street: kiss, grind, lost virginity, pregnancy, cut classes, etc. She'd been a proud Garfield Gator mom when her son played for the youth community football team. This was before the drugs consumed her life. Now life in her hood wasn't the same. Drugs and gangs had taken over. There used to be grass in every yard, fences, and clothes lines in each backyard. Now none of that was there. It wasn't the same. Still, when Denean brought up moving to Jocelyn, her response was, "Hell no." It was her hood and she loved it.

Now as she sat alone after taking both her daughters to school, she thought about what Denean said. If her children and unborn grandson had a chance in life, moving provided them with a greater chance.

Derrick hadn't gone to school that day. It was nearing graduation. He'd be moving on to tenth grade. On top of that, he had some shit he had to handle. He entered the kitchen and saw his mom at the table crying. "What's wrong?" he asked, worried.

"It's not the same," she said as she wiped her tears.

He had no idea what she was talking about. "What ain't the same?"

"Everything. Nothing. Garfield ain't the same place I grew up."

Derrick agreed with her. A lot of shit had changed in his fourteen years. He couldn't imagine how much had changed in her twenty-seven years. Realizing his mom wasn't crying over any serious drama, he got the Captain Crunch off the top of the refrigerator and poured himself a big bowl. He was hungry as hell. He took out the gallon of milk and sat down across from his mom. "Why you saying that?"

"Maybe it's time for us to move."

He'd just put a spoonful of cereal in his mouth. He shook his head in disagreement. "Move for what?"

She knew he loved Garfield as much as she did. "It's getting too dangerous up here."

"It's dangerous everywhere, Mom. You can't run from your destiny," he explained as soon as he finished chewing.

She agreed with him there. God had a plan for everyone. What she refused to accept is that you couldn't improve the chances for yourself and your children to live to an age when they'd really be considered an elder; that you couldn't move them from a place where gunfire and death was commonplace. A lot of people residing on Cornwall had simply lost their desire to do something with themselves. Many had no jobs, were supported by welfare, and spent their days and nights doing too much of nothing. Sad but true in Jocelyn's eyes. That wasn't to say all the residents were that way. Just too many.

"When you were younger, you used to tell me all the time what you wanted to do when you got older. It's been a long time since I heard any of your dreams. Why?"

He had plenty of plans. They weren't the same ones he had as a child. He recalled telling his mom he'd be the first one in his family to go to and complete college, and vowed that he'd never go on welfare or be on any type of housing assistance. He thought he'd do something in sports, but he already decided he wasn't going to go out for any team in tenth grade. Shit changed, and shit happened. He really didn't have an answer for her. "Everything is still straight, Mom."

"That's not an answer. What do you intend to do with your life?"

"Live it," he replied simply. That's all he wanted to do is live his life day to day—because tomorrow's not promised—not to anyone.

"You got a son coming into the world. There is more to think about than yourself. God forbid you get busted and go to jail." She couldn't even bring herself to say "killed."

To him that was all a part of the game—a part of the life he had chosen for himself. Keeping it a hundred, the life forced upon him. He never wanted to sell drugs. His fucked up circumstances forced him down that road. He accepted it all for what it was. "I ain't going to jail, and I ain't doing this forever. I got some plans."

"Tell me them," Jocelyn encouraged.

Sitting at the table with his mom that morning, Derrick told her his dream of making a change in Garfield and how he intended on doing it.

~ ~ ~

Anxiety—Denean thought she was too young to suffer from it, but the closer she got to her due date, July 22, the worse the attacks came. She knew she'd been snapping about stupid stuff lately, but she couldn't control it. The doctor told her this was normal behavior for first-time moms. You couldn't convince anyone in the Wright household of that. Once she'd even snapped at Rochelle, making both Chelle and Mika keep a safe distance. Derrick caught it the worst. He couldn't figure out what he did to her. "Dag, stay still," she told him.

He was trying to, but not only was she pulling the fuck out of his hair, he was also playing Madden on PlayStation. At the moment he was playing the Colts in the AFC Championship game. The winner went on to the Super Bowl. He was up 29-22, but Payton Manning and his Colts now had the ball on the seventeen yard line with thirty-four seconds remaining and no timeouts. After playing a sixteen-game season, his Steelers were a perfect 16-0 and 1-0 in the playoffs. He had to focus. "Hold up, gorgeous."

"Oh shit."

He thought she was watching the game. It appeared Manning was about to hit Marvin Harrison for a touchdown.

"My water broke."

He hit pause just as Manning released the ball. He was seated on the floor between her legs getting his hair braided. He quickly turned and saw the couch and her pants wet. "It's only the eleventh," he pointed out.

She mashed his head away so she could get up. Her stomach was huge. She hated it now. All she wanted to do is push her baby out and get her body back. She wasn't going to waste any words on Derrick's stupid ass. "Mom," she called out. "My water just broke."

Jocelyn, followed by both of her daughters, rushed down the steps. "My nephew is coming!" Rochelle exclaimed.

"Yeah!" Mika added.

Still on the floor in a daze, Derrick revealed, "He ain't due till the twenty-second."

The comment made Denean upset. She kicked the PlayStation box. The game ejected and the screen went blue. The game would have to be played over, just when he thought he was going to win. It looked like Troy Polamolu was closing in on the pass.

Now he'd never know. He was ready to say something, but her expression stopped him. He jumped up. "I'll get the bag."

July 12, 2005 at 5:51 p.m. Derrick Wright Junior was born. Eight pounds and four ounces.

Standing there watching his son come into the world, Derrick realized his mom and Denean were right. If something happened to his son, he'd kill whoever was responsible.

Two weeks after his son was born, Derrick gave his mom enough money to buy a house in Stanton Heights—not too far from Denean's parents. With his son in his arms watching the movers unload the truck, Derrick decided this was it for him. After he got rid of the two kilos of work he had left, he was getting out of the game. He had more than enough money. Life couldn't have been better for Derrick and his family.

T WELVE

L ife became boring for Jocelyn. She absolutely adored her grandson and the time the two spent together. But with her daughters, Derrick, and Denean all in school, she had a lot of free time on her hands. The decision to get her GED came as a result of wanting more for herself. She also wanted to set an example for her kids. If she could do it, as an ex-crackhead, then they had no excuse. Bettering herself was her entire focus. The furthest thing from her mind was a man.

"I know you from somewhere, shorty."

She was trying to ignore him, but the nigga who had stared at her from the other side of the room was now standing close to the chair she was sitting in. There was no way she could continue to ignore him. The dental office waiting room wasn't that big. Besides, her and the strangers in front of her—a white woman and a child around nine or ten—were the only two others waiting to see the dentist.

Jocelyn looked up at him. "I don't think so." She was tired of lame niggas coming at her with weak lines. Since she stopped smoking, niggas came at her sideways thinking that it was like it was. Naw, she was cool on that. The last time she had had sex was a few days prior to the last time she got high.

"I'm pretty sure."

She wanted to cuss his ass out, and she might have if the receptionist hadn't called her name. She got up, leaving him with a confused look on his face. He had to get at her when she was strung out on crack. Pitiful, she thought as she walked through the doors leading her to the back.

~ ~ ~

Outside on the steps in front of the Connelly Building where she was studying for her GED, Jocelyn looked up, searching for Denean's truck. Denean was running late as usual. Several cars and trucks were stopping in front of the school picking different people up, so Jocelyn didn't pay any attention to the silver and black Cutlass that stopped on Bedford Avenue.

"Excuse me, Jocelyn."

She looked into the car expecting to at least know the person calling her, but she didn't recognize him—at least not initially. Then he smiled and it came to her. He was the same nigga from the dentist office. What the hell was he, a stalker? She wasn't too worried about him trying anything. Not only were there too many people out, but also if it looked like he was getting out of his car, she'd get up and get ghost. One thing she hadn't ever been was slow.

"Told you I knew you from somewhere. I go here too. Taking up refrigerator, air duct, and air conditioner repair."

That was nice, she thought, but what the hell did that have to do with her? So she was wrong in thinking he was implying he knew her in her crack smoking days. Oh well. Luckily Denean pulled up right next to this stranger's car. "Oh, okay," she said. She got up and ignored him as he said something.

"Who was that, Mom?" Denean asked.

She shrugged. She really didn't know and didn't care.

"He's kinda cute. You sure—"

What she thought; as she turned up the car stereo drowning out whatever Denean was saying was, that she didn't want nor need a man.

~ ~ ~

It was the last day of swimming in the city, and Jocelyn promised her kids they could go. She really didn't plan on walking the lower half of the reservoir, and she, along with her two daughters, Denean, and her grandson in his stroller, had all broken out in a heavy sweat.

"I'm burning up," Tamika complained.

"Thought we was going swimming," Rochelle pointed out.

"We are."

Denean asked what the two sisters wanted to. "When we stopping?" Since the birth of her son, she had lost some of the extra weight she gained during her pregnancy. But fuck that, Jocelyn was on some other shit. Losing it all at the cause of passing out just wasn't worth it to Denean. D Jr.'s fat ass didn't make it any easier. She never though walking and pushing a stroller could be so tiring. She was exhausted.

"Two more times around and then we'll stop."

Denean and the girls stopped right then, and Jocelyn marched in place. Two more times around, and Denean wouldn't only pass out, but she was also sure she'd die. "Man, I'm done." She sat down on the grass beside the road.

Jocelyn knew Denean wasn't getting back up. "Are y'all finished too?" The girls both dropped down next to Denean in the grass.

She took ahold of her grandson's stroller. "Come on, Buddabutt, workout with Nana."

"She crazy," Chelle observed.

Again, adding what neither of the girls could, Denean said, "Crazy as hell." She fell back onto her back and stared up into the sky, exhausted to the max.

Not having to slow up so they could keep up with her, Jocelyn made good time around the reservoir. On her last lap, she told Denean to go ahead and drive down; she planned on walking. It wasn't that far of a distance and was mainly downhill.

"Why I keep running into you?"

Jocelyn looked to her right and saw the guy who claimed to attend school with her.

She never stopped her stride down the hill, having no intention of stopping and talking to him. In his car, he kept easy pace with her. "Look," she said as she stopped, planning on cussing him out. But as she looked into his car, she saw the two prettiest girls she ever saw in her life strapped in their car seats in the back. Twins. They had on matching swimsuits, oversized sun glasses framing their face, and such a "who is this woman" look on their faces, she had to smile. When she was younger, she wanted twins so she could dress them alike.

"Damn, your face actually does something other than scrunch up into a mean mug. I'm surprised."

He was smiling as he said it—showing off the pearly whites. He must have gotten them cleaned at the dentist the day she first saw him. She knew he was playing and not being ignorant, but she lost her smile. "Wasn't smiling at you."

"I kinda figured that."

"Dad," one of the twins called out.

"We want to go swimming," the other finished. To add emphasis on her words, she kicked the back of his seat several times.

"We almost there, and stop kicking my seat before I beat you."

The girls giggled and then said as one, "Yeah right!"

He turned and looked at Jocelyn. "Hope when your son starts to talk, he isn't as mouthy as these two."

She could tell that he had a very close relationship with his girls. "He's my grandson."

He found that hard to believe. He guessed she really didn't

want to be bothered. "See you around some time," he said before pulling away.

She watched him pull off, thinking "sooner than you think."

"Stalker," he said as she walked by him.

She could feel his eyes burning into her back. At that moment, walking without stumbling was the hardest thing she ever had to do. One foot in front of the other, she told herself.

Walking beside her, Denean glanced back over her shoulder at the man that spoke. "Was he talking to you?"

"No."

"You didn't know him?" She turned to look at him again. "He's the same one from that day I picked you up from school, isn't he?"

Jocelyn found an unoccupied spot in the grass, stretched out her large beach towel, and sat down on it. Out of her large bag, she pulled sun blocker, a novel by one of her favorite Publishers, Good2go Publishing, and her sun glasses, which she put on. "Hand me the baby and y'all can go get in." Right now she just wanted to relax.

Denean really wanted some answers, but knew that she wasn't going to get any. Besides, she needed to cool off in the water. She gave Jocelyn her sleeping son and quickly jumped into the pool. Rachelle was only a second behind her.

"Try it so I can whop your little ass," Jocelyn told her youngest as it appeared that Tamika was about to jump in.

"I can swim, Mommy," she whined.

The look Jocelyn gave her was enough to send her toward the kiddy pool. Both her daughters were very good swimmers. When she got in, she'd allow her youngest to get in with her. Right now, she planned on lying back and reading a few pages. It wasn't long before she sat the book aside and shut her eyes.

"Can I hold him?" The question caused her to jump.

Whoever was talking was right next to her.

Even before Jocelyn's eyes opened, she knew the voice belonged to a little girl. She sat up and lifted her sunglasses, perching them on top of her head.

"D'Naija, what did I tell you about talking to strangers?"

Jocelyn turned her head and saw the girl's father and her twin sister making his way toward her. All she could think about was he was corny as hell for this stunt.

The adorable girl looked up at her father with a confused look on her face. "You said she was your friend from grown-up school, Daddy."

Jocelyn smiled slightly. Served his two-timing ass right. He probably told them that to keep them from running back to their mom and telling her he was talking to another woman, she thought. "Oh, so I'm your friend now?"

"They asked who you were."

"Mommy," Tamika said as she rushed over being nosey. The three small girls eyed each other up.

"Yours?"

"Yes, and the one running over here now." He turned and saw Rochelle running in spite of the no running rule. "She's my pit bull."

He believed it and had to laugh. Not only did she resemble her mother, but she mirrored her mean mug. "If you say this one is your daughter too, I'm going to call you a fibber."

"She's my son's girlfriend and the mother to my grandson." Jocelyn could tell that he didn't believe her, but she wasn't going to explain shit. He could come to his own conclusion.

"Mom, I'm going to take them and get in the pool."

She wanted to get up and hit Denean, and his children didn't make it any better by saying, "Daddy, can we go too?"

Tamika grabbed a hand of each of the twins, and they hurried off to the kiddy pool.

He saw the way she was looking at him. He spread his arms wide. "I know how this appears, but I didn't put them up to this." He crossed his heart and raised his hand toward the sky.

It was an act she used to do with her kids. "Cross my heart and hope to die," she'd say or hear them say. It made her smile.

"Wait a minute—is that a smile? That one has to be for me."

Her grandson stirred and she used the opportunity to take her eyes off the guy's chiseled body. With the sun and water glistening, she was glad for the distraction. She patted the baby's back and he stopped fidgeting. The guy obviously thought he had game, but it wasn't that good. She glanced back up at him. "So you told your girls I was your friend so they ain't go back and snitch."

"Snitch to who?" He knew who, but he'd play her game.

"Their mother or your woman you might got both."

He chuckled. "Me telling them you were a friend had nothing to do with their mom."

She was going to say then it had to be his woman he was afraid of finding out. Whatever the case, it didn't have shit to do with Jocelyn. He could cheat to his heart's content. It just would not be with her.

"Wait. If you are trying to ask me if I have a girlfriend, the answer is no. Their mom . . ."

"Is just your BM, right?" she stated, cutting him off.

Several kids came running by, and Jocelyn put her hand protectively over her grandson.

The stranger stood there as if ready to tackle anyone who came too close. She had to smile.

"You have a beautiful smile. Should try smiling more. And to answer your question, yeah she's only my BM."

She wanted to ask so many more questions, but there was no need. What did it matter? She knew he was lying. She couldn't recall one man in her life that was honest. Oh, they said all the right things in the beginning. As soon as they got the coochie, they got sloppy with the lies. Right now she was focused on getting her GED and then studying to be a paralegal. She didn't have the time for a man.

"And if you wondering why she isn't here right now, I can answer that too. She's at her crib getting ready to go out to the club."

Jocelyn laughed, and then she saw the expression on his face. It was a little after 2:00 p.m. "You can't be serious."

"No, I'm lying. The bit—I mean woman just might be getting in from the club last night. With her, there is no telling."

It was only Tuesday. Even when she did go out, who went out Monday night?

She could see she had hit a sensitive spot. "Sorry."

"It's cool. She ain't shit as a woman or mother, but she gave me the two most important people in my life." He looked toward his girls. "I'm George, but everyone calls me Gee."

She shook his hand. "Are they your only two?"

He nodded. "That really isn't your grandson, is it?"

It was her turn to nod, and then the two began to tell each other about themselves. Jocelyn even told him the embarrassing fact that she got high for eight years. She wasn't sure how he'd take it, but she didn't want him to find out later.

"I sold drugs longer than that, and I ain't proud of that. It's not where you been, mami, but where you going. Right now my life revolves around my girls and school. I need a good woman by my side."

Keeping it a hundred, Jocelyn realized he had her long before he asked for her number.

~ ~ ~

Asking her son to watch his sisters wasn't as easy as it used to be when she was strung out on crack. Before, she'd be halfway out the door when she told him to watch them. Explaining to him why she needed him wasn't easy and was something new to her.

She didn't know what his reaction would be. That she was actually going out on a date was strange even for her. It wasn't a hookup—a sex for crack thing. It was a real date for dinner, followed by a Monday night football game—Steelers vs. Baltimore Ravens at the stadium. It would be her first time seeing her favorite team live. The anticipation that she'd be at the stadium dimmed in comparison to the fact that she was actually going on a date.

Somehow her son found out who George was just from what she told him. He told her he was respected in the streets, was raising his two daughters, and was retired from the game. He also told her he had a jealous and crazy baby mom, and advised her to be careful. The last thing she was was a punk. She wasn't looking for trouble, but wouldn't run from it if it came her way.

~ ~ ~

Two days before Thanksgiving, the Wright family got the surprise of their lives.

Jocelyn, George, his daughters, her girls and grandson, and Denean were all in the living room watching the new Lion King movie. As baby Simba was on the verge of being trampled, someone rang the doorbell. Being the closest, Jocelyn got up to see who it was. Standing at her door was a young girl holding a baby. "Yes?"

"Does Derrick Wright live here?"

Her eyes traveled from the woman to the baby she had

bundled in her arms. All she thought about at that moment was, "I hope this isn't another grandchild."

Hearing a female voice asking for her man, Denean got up to see who it was. Her thoughts ran similar to Jocelyn's at the sight of the girl and the baby. If Derrick had stepped out and had another baby, Denean was fucking him up along with the bitch who now stood in front of her.

"My son's name is Derrick Wright. Who are you?"

The woman smiled as tears began to fall from her eyes. "My father always went for the gorgeous ones."

Jocelyn stared at her, confused, and then her hand shot to her mouth as the realization of who stood in front of her was. "Oh my God!" It had been a long time, but she had seen the girl once before when she was two or three—had even done her hair. But this couldn't be real.

The movie was forgotten as everyone looked on at the exchange between the two at the door.

"My name is—"

"India," Jocelyn finished for her in disbelief. The two embraced as they cried. Denean had no idea who India was, but once it was revealed that she was Derrick's older sister, she too began to cry. She knew he had a sister and two brothers he'd never seen before. In the midst of their reunion, she called his phone. "Sexy, you need to come home. You need to come home right now." She didn't explain things, just hung up.

T HIRTEEN

G etting out of the drug game wasn't as easy as he thought. For almost two years, that's all he knew every single day—taking no days off. It was his job, morning, noon, and night. Saying he was done wasn't the same as being done. His work began to dwindle and he had the urge to re-up. People called him putting in orders that he couldn't fill. Tre even called him wondering why he hadn't called in a minute. As his money piled up, so did Tre's since he still got his work from him. The only thing about this job was there was no retirement party. No going-away bash. When he got down to his last three ounces, he decided to give them to Michelle. That's why he was up on Cornwall Street opening her front door.

As usual, it was unlocked. Something as simple as locking her front door now was overlooked. The housing authority offered to move her into another house, but she refused. She rarely left her home, and when she did, it was always with Derrick to the same destination: the cemetery where Kelly was buried.

"Hey, babe," she sat in her bedroom, crack all over the place.

He smiled, but had to hold his breath as he crossed the room and opened the window, letting in some air. Between her funk and the foul and identifiable smell of crack cocaine being smoked, the room stank.

He tried to get over to see her a couple times a week, but got caught up the last week getting rid of all his work. His son also caught a bad cold, sending him rushing to the hospital, fearful that it was something worse.

Michelle pulled at her clothes and attempted to straighten her tangled hair. Truth be told, she no longer cared about her appearance. Getting high consumed her days because only then did she not have to think about her daughter being dead. She missed her terribly. Her fingers and lips were black from being burnt from the hot crack pipe. The only time any of that mattered was when Derrick came around.

He hated seeing her in the condition she was in; tried everything he could think of to get her to see she was killing herself. She refused to go into rehab; wouldn't even hear him out when he told her he'd pay for everything. He'd done his research and was going to send her to the Betty Ford Rehabilitation Facility, one of the best in the country. He didn't like giving her crack, especially now, and told her he wasn't giving her any more initially after she got out of the hospital. She cried and begged so much that he finally gave in. The guilt he felt for the whole affair—her drug use, and Kelly's death—ate at him.

She giggled. "Stinks in here, huh?"

He smiled. "You think? I bought you something to eat. Come on and get up and go wash your hands."

She sat there with the pipe in her left hand and a lighter in her right, staring up at him with a blank expression on her face. The scent of the food he carried in with him reached her nostrils, causing her stomach to rumble. She hadn't really eaten much since she last saw him. She let both items fall onto the bed and got to her feet. Tears began to run down her face. "Do you miss her, Derrick?"

He nodded, not trusting himself to speak right then.

Michelle smiled in spite of her tears and crossed the room and hugged him. She knew he wouldn't shy away from her funk. He never did. "I love you, Derrick," she told him.

His own eyes were watery as he said, "I love you too." He

really did.

After he made her eat, he had her get in the tub. Michelle wanted to visit her daughter's gravesite, and he agreed to take her. Kelly was buried in the cemetery they had to pass every day on their way to Arsenal Middle School. As he drove down Penn Avenue after going to Hallmark Greetings in Bloomfield on Liberty Avenue to get some balloons and flowers, his cell phone went off letting him know a call was coming through. He saw "Gorgeous" displayed across the screen. "What's up?"

His entire expression changed as he listened to Denean. He dropped his phone into his lap and made an illegal U-turn, nearly causing an accident. He ignored all the horns as he sped back up Penn Avenue. As the light turned red, Derrick went right through it. His mind was on the call he just got from his woman. He could tell she was crying. He couldn't help but think some nigga held her at gunpoint. Ever since Kelly's death, he had that fear. He retrieved his gun from under his seat and gripped it tightly as he thought of his family. If something happened to any member of his family, whoever was responsible would die. He put that on his dead homie Sparks.

Michelle rode silently, asking no questions. Although she didn't know what was going on, she knew it had to be something serious. She just hoped it wasn't as serious as it seemed.

When he stopped in front of his home, he didn't even bother shutting his car door or attempting to conceal the gun he held in his hands.

The front door opened, and he saw his mom holding who he mistakenly thought was his son. She was smiling. When Denean stepped beside his mom actually holding his son, he wondered who his mom was holding. He slowed his approach. Seeing they were in no danger, he slipped his gun into his jacket pocket.

"Who is in the car?"

"Michelle, what's up?" He wondered why Denean called him with that message.

Jocelyn told her she shouldn't have called him saying what she did. She knew he'd automatically think something was wrong. Seeing him put away his gun, she was correct in her assumption. "Tell her to get out the car and come in." Michelle had not only been a person Jocelyn occasionally got high with, but the two had grown up together and were friends. She knew the story about Kelly's death and the fact that the people who killed her were after the drugs Derrick stashed there. She also knew about her son's guilt over Kelly's death.

He went back to his car, told Michelle to get out, and closed the car door.

Besides going to her daughter's gravesite, she hadn't gone anywhere else since getting out of the hospital. She hesitated briefly until Derrick told her it was okay. Light rain fell from the sky.

After hugging Michelle a long moment, Jocelyn, with her arm around her frail friend, entered her home. Derrick followed them.

"Surprise!" his two sisters screamed in unison.

Derrick stood just inside the door, wondering what was going on and who the baby his mom held and the woman standing by the TV were. Tears rolled down her cheeks.

"Oh my God! He looks just like LaRon," the woman exclaimed.

He had no clue who LaRon was, and he didn't know who the girl who resembled Gabrielle Union was either. She was so beautiful that if he had met her before, he never would have forgotten her face. Even if she wasn't crying, he probably would have stared at her. He watched her cross the room, and returned her hug awkwardly. Over her shoulder, he looked at

Denean and his mom's boyfriend, Gee—both of whom were smiling. He was waiting for Ashton Kutcher of Punk'd to come running out or dude from Twilight Zone. Derrick had no clue what the fuck was going on.

"You look just like your brother," the woman said as she stepped away and looked up at him.

This really was some weird shit. He didn't have a brother. And then it hit him. His heart began to race. He had trouble breathing. He did have a brother. In fact, he had two of them and a sister.

"I'm your sister, Derrick. My name is India," she explained.

He'd dreamed and fantasized about his three other siblings from his father.

His mom told him about them, but he had long since given up hope of ever meeting them. Yet, here one of them stood. He felt lightheaded, on the verge of passing out. It felt like a dream. He crushed her to his chest in a powerful embrace that lasted several minutes, and when they broke apart, had them laughing and crying in happiness.

Jocelyn looked on crying as well. The smile she'd seen on India's face had looked so familiar before she learned who the girl was, because it was identical to her son's.

"What up wit my brothers? Where they at?" He sat down next to his older sister, allowing her to hold his hands.

"LaRon, the one you could pass as his twin, is nineteen. Balil is seventeen, and I'm the oldest at twenty—soon to be twenty-one on November ninth. I wasn't sure how you'd feel about us, so I came alone to see."

He took the baby his mom held from her. "Who dis, my neph? Yours?"

"Hell no. He's your nephew, but LaRon's son. I don't have any kids and won't have any til I'm married and established."

She took out her cell phone and called LaRon, who had been waiting on the call, and told them to come on. "They're right in East Liberty, so it's not going to take them long."

While she'd waited for Derrick to come, she had learned a little about her baby brother. His life was similar to LaRon's. Thankfully Derrick was exiting the game. Hustling was all LaRon knew. and she doubted he'd ever stop. She took the blame for LaRon's hustler mentality. At the time, she felt they had few options. Some days, like this one, she wished she had.

Derrick parted the curtains and kept his eyes glued on the streets, waiting for his brothers to pull up. When the shiny black Cadillac Escalade stopped right by the driveway, he was out of his seat and out the door. A female was behind the wheel, but he saw the two dudes as they got out. He recognized LaRon immediately. His sister was right, they looked alike. Balil was the first one to reach him, and the two hugged as they both cried.

LaRon looked up as his baby bro came out of the house. He was taken aback at how much they looked alike. He couldn't wait for his turn to hug his bro, and he wrapped his arms around both Balil and Derrick, who were already locked in a brotherly embrace.

Everyone came out of the house and watched the exchange between the brothers. India explained who the girl behind the wheel was. "Her name is Deamber, LaRon's BM and constant shadow. Poor girl hardly leaves his side."

Jocelyn laughed. She recalled how she stayed at Derrick's father's side while they were together. Denean was the same way. It was something about the men in their family.

Denean didn't see what was wrong with that. She'd remain at Derrick's side.

Finally the brothers broke apart. "You out here doing big things, bro. Is this you?" Derrick asked, indicating the

Escalade.

LaRon nodded. His business was the streets. Although he was from Wilkinsburg, his range stretched further than its lines. Once they got his bro's name and found out he was from Garfield, it didn't take long for him to find out all about him. He was impressed. "From what I hear, young nigga, you ain't doing too bad yourself."

Derrick didn't try to deny it. His life had changed dramatically since he started selling at thirteen. In a few months, he'd be fifteen. He had a nice bit of change stashed. Naw, he wasn't doing too bad.

India went down to join her brothers, and the four of them did a group hug. She was happy, but her happiness wouldn't be complete until she located the two youngest of her father's children—two sisters. When she got the letter from her dad, a man she didn't know, initially she thought, fuck him! He hadn't done shit for her or her brothers. Now that he was on his death bed (he had colon cancer), he wanted to see them. She decided to go—not because he was dying inside of New Jersey State Prison, but because her family meant everything to her. Finding out about his other kids was the one reason she went. She got the moms' names and went from there. Now her dad was gone, but she had found one of her siblings already.

"Nigga, you ain't even fifteen yet," Balil pointed out.

CYS getting involved in their life changed Derrick's entire life. He knew he never would have sold one drug if the CYS caseworker hadn't threatened to take him and his sisters and split them up. The family walked back into the house where they spent the next three hours filling each other in on their lives.

Denean took everyone, including Michelle, to Kelly's gravesite and then to Boston Market in Shadyside, leaving the four siblings at the house. She knew how much Derrick wanted to meet his brothers and sisters. This meant a lot to him, and it meant a lot to her. They planned on getting married on his sixteenth birthday. He'd already given her an engagement ring. She couldn't wait for the day she'd become his wife. Her parents had come around, accepting that she loved Derrick, and had given their blessings on the engagement. Things were perfect.

Derrick didn't want his brothers and sister to go. India left around midnight explaining that she had an important exam the following morning. Derrick was kinda shocked his sis was attending Duquesne University and was studying to be an attorney.

At three in the morning, his brothers bounced. If his son didn't have an appointment in the morning at ten, he would have gone with them. Lying on his back next to Denean, he thought about the fact his father was gone. He never recalled ever seeing him. He didn't hate him, but he still felt no sadness over the news he was dead. The man was a stranger. So were his older siblings. At least they now had the opportunity to get to know one another. India was right when she said, "Dad done six good things if nothing else, had the six of us." Derrick could think of one more good thing: contacting India before he died and telling her about his other kids.

After Derrick took his son to his appointment, he had plans to meet up and spend the day with his siblings. Denean mumbled something in her sleep, grabbed his arm, and draped it across her body as she nestled back into him. It was the usual way they slept. He smiled as he held her. Life was good. He couldn't wait to kick it with his siblings in a few hours. LaRon told him he had something special to show him. He would find out what it was soon.

Being with his siblings, especially his brothers, was like a dream. They spent most of the next few days together.

His brother LaRon was the one with the money, but it was India who ran shit.

"There's only going to be one street pharmacist in this family," she informed them one day. "And if you are wondering, yes, Derrick, I'm talking to you. I heard you are out of the drug game. Good. But being around LaRon, you might get the itch to jump back in. I'm telling you and I'm telling LaRon, I'm not having it. Am I understood?"

He smiled as LaRon told her he heard her. Derrick wasn't so quick to agree. It had been a long time since he truly listened to anyone. That wasn't something he was used to.

He was officially out of the game. Intent and focused on graduating from high school and going to college. He had no money worries. In fact, he talked to an older nigga from the hood, Darrell Reed, and he was going to put him on to investing his money—possibly buying some rental property. He didn't want to get back in anyway. "I hear you."

The downtown condo India owned was bought and paid for by LaRon. "All she does is spend all my money," LaRon joked.

She spent, but Derrick soon found out, she couldn't spend all his brother's money.

It came in at a high turnover rate. The two kilos and couple ounces he nearly lost to Steve—his whole stash—wouldn't have even covered LaRon's daily quota he put out. When he went to one of his stash spots and saw the keys of powder—too many to count by sight—he also noticed the quality.

"You got a Cuban connect, Bro?"

"Columbian," LaRon corrected him. "Only the best."

Derrick was introduced to the top soldiers on what LaRon called "his" team. LaRon explained that only a few of his men had ever seen his face, and only one of them could ever lay claim to actually getting coke from him: his woman's older brother, Curtis, his closest friend and top boss. It was true.

After he was taken out to East Bumba Fuck, a place called Altoona, Pennsylvania, Derrick wanted back in. Now he saw why his bro had a picture of Al Pacino from Scarface on his arm and why everyone called him "the Black Scarface." Inside a safe that was hidden behind a huge bookshelf, was a safe as big as a bank safe. When LaRon opened the safe, Derrick looked at all the money in amazement. "I got pennies to your millions."

LaRon replied, "12-4-17 and soon to be 20 as soon as I program it in." He pushed several electronic buttons, causing there to be some loud beeps and then silence. "It's done."

Derrick had no idea what those numbers were. Couldn't be what he thought they were. "What's that?"

LaRon shut the safe. "It's all of our birthdays and the combo to the safe. What's mine is yours, Bro." As LaRon told him that, he handed Derrick a key to the mansion they now stood in.

Derrick couldn't believe it. "How much is in there?"

LaRon shrugged. "Last time I counted, in '03. It was over $7 mil."

Yeah, his bro was on a whole other level. His interest was reawakened. He wanted to get on his brother's level. All he had to do was figure out how to convince LaRon to allow it, and worse even how to tell India his college plans were on hold.

After sitting around India's condo stuffed from the dinner she cooked, India made an announcement. "From now on, no matter what else is going on in our lives, every Wednesday we all meet up here for dinner. Just us."

Stretched out on the floor, Derrick nodded. He wasn't done asking questions. He couldn't believe they'd grown up in Wilkinsburg and they had never crossed each other's paths.

"LaRon, this untouchable shit you think you got going on

has to end. Scarface is a movie. All the gangsters, Capone, Gotti, Frank Lucas, and all the others ended up feeling the strong arm of the law. I'm still waiting for you to tell me why you are still selling drugs."

He didn't answer her because he had no answer to give her. All he knew was he was good at it and it brought in millions. When he first got involved, it was akin to circumstances like his brothers. The only difference was Derrick came to get involved on his own, while the decision for LaRon was made by India. At the time, they had no other option. "Now that we found our lil bro, I might be getting out soon."

She heard him, but knew it was bullshit. She wasn't going to waste any more words on that matter. She had something else that needed her attention. "You got a C-minus. What the fuck is up with that?"

That caught LaRon's attention as well. "C-minus, nigga," he repeated, addressing Balil.

Balil had pulled a dining room chair into the living room and was seated, with India now standing directly in front of him. "It was on some surprise shit. He ain't even let us know there was a test. It ain't really count for—"

The rest of what he was going to say never escaped his mouth. India's first shot out and she punched him in the center of his chest. Balil toppled backward and landed hard on his back. The plush carpet softened his fall, but the punch still hurt. "It ain't really count," she said, mimicking her brother. "What the hell you mean it ain't count? He graded it, so it counted. How many times do I got to tell you, ain't nobody gonna give you shit in this world. No one is gonna give you a pass because it was a surprise. Failing in this family isn't an option. We prepare for surprises."

Derrick listened intently. Balil made no attempt to get up— just lay there rubbing his chest. Derrick did not know if he would have taken a blow like that so quietly.

"Better not see you driving your whip either, not until you bring your grade up," LaRon told him.

Balil was used to his sister's hits. He knew it was a waste of time trying to explain shit. A test was in three days. He'd ace it and be back to driving the Benz his bro bought him for his sixteenth birthday. He hated buses, but for three days, he'd be back to the big yellow one. "That hurt," he said.

Everyone laughed. Derrick already loved his family.

~ ~ ~

Nothing Derrick said convinced LaRon to go against what India said. At the moment India wasn't too pleased with him. He'd fallen way behind on his schooling. He didn't catch a body shot like Balil had, but she did show up at his school and have a lengthy talk with the principal and the guidance counselor.

"Derrick is such a smart young man," the counselor said. "He's just not dedicating himself to his studies."

"Trust me, he'll start to," India vowed.

"She's like our mom, Bro. The only difference is she doesn't take any shit," Balil told Derrick when he told his brothers about India showing up at the school.

"You'll get used to her. It's best not to cross her," LaRon advised, "or go against her wishes."

Derrick was beginning to see that.

"Sexy, why can't I bowl? I'm not even showing right now," Denean pointed out.

"India said you can't," Derrick told her—not bothering to elaborate any further. To him, nothing else needed to be said.

Denean entered the room from the private bathroom in their bedroom, in just her bra and a pair of Apple Bottoms jeans. "If you wouldn't have ran your mouth, she never would have known. I'm not even showing."

He guessed she was right. He had no idea India would forbid Denean and Deamber, who also was pregnant, from bowling. He tried to rub her stomach, but Denean smacked his hand away, causing him to laugh.

"Ain't nothing funny, D. You know I love to bowl." She paused before saying, "I'm going to bowl anyways."

Derrick turned up his lips in a look of disbelief.

"What? I'm grown as hell. If I wanna bowl, I'll bowl."

He turned away and put on some cologne. He wasn't going to entertain her foolishness. They both knew she wasn't going to go against India.

"You think I'm scared? I ain't even listen to my parents." She realized Derrick wasn't paying her too much attention. "Can you please talk to her for me? Tell her I'll be careful," she begged.

Derrick laughed, causing Denean to slap him hard on his back. In the short time he'd known his sister India, he realized no one went against her. Denean wouldn't bowl, and there wasn't anything either of them could do about it.

"I hate you!" she called out as she went down the steps.

"Love you too, gorgeous," he said through his laughter.

It was a family outing a day before his fifteenth birthday. At least that's what Derrick was told. Denean, unable to keep it to herself, told him it was really a surprise birthday party for him.

"Remember to act surprised," she warned him as they neared the bowling lane up North Versailles off of Ardmore Boulevard.

"She told him," everyone said as Derrick overdid it with acting surprised.

Still in all, they did enjoy themselves. India even allowed

Denean and Deamber to bowl a little. By the time Derrick blew out the candles on his cake, it was a little after midnight. Time to get up out of there. LaRon, Balil and Derrick were going out to the eighteen and older club on the South Side.

"I'll swing past and snatch you up after I get showered and changed," LaRon informed him out in the parking lot before they drove off.

Denean kissed him at the door. "Don't have me fuck up one of them slut buckets, D."

"Stop trippin'. Love you," he told her as he left out. He was still laughing and smiling as he got in LaRon's truck.

"What's funny?"

"Denean's pregnant."

He got a text: "Remember that when one of them bitches get their funky ass all up against you. Love you too. Have fun."

He laughed even more. "She be trippin' 'bout them bitches. She ain't have shit to worry about." His creeping days were over.

"Tonight is your night, nigga. It's our first time together on your B-day. We gonna let our shit swing."

"Fifteen and already shittin' on niggas. Happy birthday, lil Bro," Balil said from the backseat.

Derrick dapped his brother up, and when he turned back around, LaRon held a long platinum chain and a diamond Jesus emblem in his hand.

"Damn, Bro." Derrick knew the chain cost a nice bit of change.

"Happy Birthday, nigga. Got something nice for you in the a.m." LaRon hugged Derrick, knowing his bro would love the Kawasaki motorcycle he had for him, still at the dealer's. "Hop in the back and enjoy my gift to you on top of this chain."

"Happy Birthday, Derrick," the twins said.

The brown-skin shorties popped up, causing Derrick to

jump. He wasn't going to accept this gift. This was what Denean was talking about. Before he had a chance to decline, the twins pulled him into the back. He didn't put up much of a fight, but he did tell them to hold up. It wasn't his fault they didn't listen. By the time Balil jumped up front, one twin was giving him head and the other was licking his balls. "Drive, nigga." The last thing he needed was for Denean to walk down the row and catch him—especially since it felt so good.

LaRon laughed, and as he pulled away, he turned up the sounds to cover up the slurping and sucking going on in the back.

~ ~ ~

His head was spinning by the time he stepped out in the cool morning air at 5:00 a.m. The party didn't really get started until after 2:00 a.m. when the door locked and everything was free. LaRon even hired some top-notch exotic dancers, flown in from out of state. Every woman in the club, and some of those had niggas, wanted to ride with the three. Not only was Derrick not with it, but also he'd done more than enough for a lifetime in the cheating department this night. Besides, Denean's final text sealed his night: "You better be here before the sun rises. Love you."

He had no idea when sunrise was, but he intended on being in before it arrived.

A lot of people mingled outside the club, a lot of whom were still looking for their hookup or were cementing the deal. No one wanted to go home alone. Really, no one wanted the night to end.

"Balil, let's ride," LaRon called out to his bro.

Balil was taking a number down from a slim brown-skinned shorty. She didn't have too much body, but she resembled Jada Pinkett-Smith. He had to smash the woman that went by the name Caramel. He didn't know if that was her real name, and didn't give a fuck. He'd had a thing for Jada since Set It Off.

LaRon sobered up immediately when he felt the cool air. He hadn't drunk as much as either of his brothers, knowing he had to drive.

Balil finished up and made his way over to his brothers. He draped his arm around his baby bro and teased him. "Denean's gonna kick your ass, nigga."

"Naw, I'm cool." He said it, but he looked up. There wasn't any sun yet.

Turning back as Derrick stumbled with the drunk shit, LaRon was about to say something, when he noticed two niggas coming their way with a determined stride. Years of being on the streets had honed his instincts. The niggas were up to no good. Before anyone, including the niggas stalking them, knew it, LaRon had his gun in his hand and pushed past a startled Balil and Derrick, with his 9mm raised. "Life or death, niggas. Y'all make the call," he said, his voice steady.

When his brother pushed by him, Derrick wobbled into a car. He regained his balance just as he heard LaRon's words. He watched as two niggas let the guns they had pointed harmlessly at the ground, clatter to the pavement. He sobered up immediately.

People close enough to see what was going on scrambled to get far away from the deadly scene.

"Smart choice," LaRon told them. It wasn't the first time niggas tried to get at him. Up to that point, none had been successful. "Empty them pockets, bitch niggas, and you better pray something falls to the ground besides lint."

Derrick was heated. Before either of his brothers could stop him, he sucker punched one of the niggas. The guy immediately fell and went out cold. "You want what we got. Think you can take it, pussies?"

Derrick reached for his brother's gun, but LaRon didn't let him have it, and Balil picked up the nigga dropped to the ground. "Let me kill these niggas, bro," he begged.

Under different circumstances and with fewer potential witnesses, LaRon wouldn't have hesitated about filling the niggas with holes. All he did now was backhand the nigga still standing, with his strap. "They ain't worth it, Bro." He kept his eyes on both niggas as he and his brothers made their way to his truck.

"Damn, lil Bro. You got that one-hitter quitter," LaRon joked.

Despite being mad as hell, Derrick laughed. "Them niggas should be in another world right now for trying to jack us."

LaRon agreed, but niggas that acted off anger always ended up with the shit end of the stick. "We'll cross their path again."

Derrick disagreed with his brother there. They should have settled shit right then. Allowing slimy-ass niggas to skate was only asking for problems. "You should have let me kill 'em, Bro."

Balil laughed. "Nigga a straight live wire."

Before LaRon could agree, bullets shattered the windshield. He'd sat his strap on his lap. Now he reached for it as glass fragments flew into his face. He ignored both glass and bullets as he returned fire.

At the sound of gunfire, people ran in panic trying to get away.

He shot recklessly until the clip was empty. He'd never forget what either of the niggas looked like. "Bitch niggas is dead. On my word," he promised. "Y'all cool?"

"Yeah," Balil said from the back.

"Lil, Bro, you cool?" Blood fell from LaRon's face, but he

ignored it as he turned once he didn't get a response from Derrick.

Derrick was sitting up straight in his seat. His eyes were wide open, but never again would he blink. A bullet had pierced the front of his skull, killing him instantly.

LaRon screamed in a mixture of pain and rage.

Balil stood up in the back and peered over at his little brother's lifeless form.

Their screams pierced the silence with their anguish.

F OURTEEN

L aRon refused to believe that his brother was gone. "Hang in there, Bro. Please don't die on me." He sped down Carson headed toward South Side Hospital. A police motorcade followed behind him. They commanded him to pull over, but there was no way.

"On the ground," a cop ordered as he pointed his gun on the driver's door.

Mindless of his own safety, LaRon flung his door open and pulled his brother out with him. Blinded by his tears and the bright lights from the cop cars, LaRon stood with his brother in his arms staring defiantly at the cops. If they shot and killed him because he was attempting to save his brother's life, it was a bullet he had to take. He turned and headed toward the emergency doors.

"Hold your fire," a black cop ordered. Right now he was in charge and he realized what the young male was trying to do. "Hold your fire," he repeated.

Balil came out on the other side and followed his brother into the hospital. For a Wednesday night, the emergency room was crowded.

"I need a doctor! My brother's been shot," LaRon screamed. "Please help me!"

A nurse taking a woman's vitals stopped what she was doing and reached him first. Seeing the bullet hole in his forehead, Lisa Fuller, an RN of seventeen years, knew she was looking at a corpse and not a potential patient.

More people came running out from the back. They took the body draped in the hysterical man's arms and rushed him to the back.

Lisa pained for the child. So many young black males entered the emergency room only to be carried out in a body bag. It was becoming a trend. So much so that she was seriously considering changing her profession. Right now she went on instinct. "Sir, you need to be seen as well."

LaRon felt no pain from the lacerations on his face, nor from the large piece of glass stuck in his cheek. His mind and body were numb. He tried to push the woman in front of him into the room where they'd taken his brother. "Go to my brother. Please go save my brother." That's all that mattered to him. "You should have let me kill 'em, bro." His brother's words echoed in his head. If he had, his brother would still be— No! he screamed in his head. He couldn't bring himself to say it. His brother had a chance. Doctors performed miracles all the time.

"The doctors are going to do their best for your brother, sir. You have to be seen as well," Lisa said encouragingly. She knew there was no hope for the other victim. A doctor came out to assist her.

"Call India," LaRon told his brother as he was led away by the nurse. India would make it all right. She'd know how to handle this. He believed that with his whole heart.

It was always that way. From the moment their mom died in a traffic accident when India was twelve, she'd taken on the responsibility of raising him and Balil. The only reason their mom's cousin took them in was because India promised her that they'd never be a burden. Greedy for the state-issued money for taking in the three children, Marcia agreed to take custody of them. But true to her word, India made sure she nor her brothers were a burden. She sold weed from the age of twelve to almost fourteen to get them the basic things they needed. For the money and not love had she taken them in, and she spent very little of the money on them.

"Roof over your head, food to eat, and a bed to sleep in," was her frequent comment.

That was okay because India took care of them. That is until LaRon turned twelve and she told him it was now his job to make the money. She dreamed of becoming an attorney and therefore had to focus on school. From that day on, LaRon sold drugs to provide for the three of them. But it was India who handled things when shit went wrong.

"Call India," LaRon repeated.

"Son?"

Balil turned when the man spoke. He pulled out his cell phone. "Can you tell me what happened?"

He wasn't in the streets as hard as his two brothers, but he was in them enough to know you don't talk to the jakes. "Naw." The niggas responsible for shooting at them would get dealt with.

Clyde Dexter, a lieutenant in the Zone 2 Police Department, expected nothing more. That was the normal response he received whenever he was faced with obtaining information from witnesses in a shooting or killing. The no-snitch policy in most inner-city neighborhoods would put the LA Costra Nostra to shame. It made his job so much harder. He nodded to one of his officers to follow the kid.

"Derrick's been shot!" Balil wept into the phone. "They shot, D, India."

At her home in her condo, India was trying to get her last few minutes of rest, when her cell phone began to vibrate. It couldn't be time for her to get up. She had just lay down after a long night. As the fogginess lifted, she realized it wasn't her alarm, but that someone was calling her. She pushed send, answering, and then her world came crashing down. She was getting up to when she asked, "Where is he?"

"South Side Hospital."

"I'm on my way." She grabbed her keys and purse and raced out of her home still in her pajamas. As she rode the elevator to the garage, she took assurance in Balil's words. He said he got shot—not that he was dead. She loved her brother and didn't want anything to happen to him. On the way to the hospital, she silently prayed to God that he'd be okay.

Pulling up in front of the emergency room door, she saw several cop cars lining the driveway to the entrance. She parked and noticed her brother's truck with police yellow tape surrounding it. Her heart raced even faster.

"Are you a member of the victim's family?" a newscaster with a camera man asked her.

She rushed by him and by several cops. Balil was seated in one of the waiting room chairs crying silently. "Balil."

At the sound of his sister's voice, the floodgates opened and he jumped to his feet and buried his head into her shoulder. "Some motherfuckers shot D, India," he said, his voice filled with pain.

India searched the room for her third brother. "Where's LaRon?"

It took him several attempts before he managed to say, "He's in the back. He got glass in his face."

She was relieved at the news. At least he too hadn't been shot. "Excuse me, miss."

With her brother still clutching her as though his life depended on it, India turned to face the man standing behind her. She looked at his name tag: "C. Dexter." The last thing she wanted to do was talk to a cop. "Yes?"

When India turned to face him, the cop was unable to formulate his words. Her beauty was that mesmerizing. He'd performed this task countless times, and not once had he been at a loss for words. Quickly he collected himself. After talking

155

to one of the doctors, he now knew he was dealing with a homicide. "Ma'am, are you related to the victims?" he asked. He forced himself to look into her eyes. Her nipples were pressed up against the silk of her pajama top.

India was used to making men uncomfortable. Ever since her first training bra, she had to deal with men ogling her body and face. People said she was model gorgeous.

She thought of herself as above average. But conceited she wasn't. "They are all my little brothers," she revealed.

Damn! His job had just gotten more difficult. "May I have a private word with you?"

After telling Balil to sit down, she followed the cop and stepped into a room as he held the door for her. As she waited on him to talk, her nerves already on edge, her heart rate doubled.

Clyde pulled out a small tablet and pen. "Can you give me your brothers' names and birth dates?"

She did, but she wanted some answers. She got nothing from his facial expression.

He wrote both names down before looking into her eyes. "Ma'am, I'm sorry. Your brother Derrick didn't survive."

The words erased the hope that her brothers were okay. This couldn't be real. It was his fifteenth birthday. He had gone out to celebrate. How could this happen? Before she had a chance to give it any more thought, she did something she thought only white girls did, she fainted.

~ ~ ~

"Ms. Jones, you fainted. Will you please lay there a moment?"

She had no idea how long she'd been out, but she felt fine now. Against the doctor's wishes, she sat up. As soon as she did, both brothers hugged her. Their sobs told her that she had to be strong. They needed her. She'd shown a weakness by crying. She wouldn't make that mistake again. Her time for crying would be later. "LaRon, go get your face taken care of." She could see where they started to stitch him, but he obviously made them stop so he could check on her. "Balil, pull yourself together. Derrick is gone. We have . . ."

"It's my fault. Niggas was tryin' to jack us," LaRon revealed.

India touched LaRon's chin gently and looked at her brother's face. He'd have some scars, maybe even require plastic surgery. Minor things. He was alive. "You didn't pull the trigger that killed our brother. Both of you pull it together. LaRon, go and let them treat you. Balil, go with him." She saw the cop who told her that Derrick was dead standing in the hall staring at her. She figured he wanted to ask some questions.

Until she found out what happened, no one was speaking to him.

Clyde had tried unsuccessfully to keep the two brothers out of the room while the doctors treated their sister. Now he watched as both went off to do as she said without a word. Just moments ago, he thought he was about to get into a physical altercation with them. She couldn't be too much older than her siblings, but they listened to her.

Once her brothers left, leaving her in the room with the doctor and a nurse, India, stood up. "I'm fine, Doctor."

"Ms. Jones, I think . . ."

She held up her hand. "Really I am." She walked away from them. She noticed the sergeant was about to speak. "I apologize for fainting, sir. Right now I have family to call."

He watched her walk down the hall, her head held high and a determined stride, with a certain awe. His respect for her grew. He'd make sure the best man in homicide handled the case. Clyde was scheduled to head an investigation involving a huge drug ring inside the city. His time would be limited. He couldn't stop himself from looking at her ass. She didn't have on any panties. Man, she's something special, he thought. He shook his head and averted his eyes. Stay focused, he told himself.

After checking on LaRon to make sure he was okay, India walked out to the waiting room and hugged Balil. Together they walked outside. There were more newscasters, and they all rushed at her.

Clyde was headed out planning to keep the news away from her, when she spoke. "Please don't make this any harder than it already is. I have nothing to say."

The silence that followed her words surprised him. Clyde never saw a newscaster not respond or respect a "no" comment, and essentially that's what she just gave them.

Trying not to look at her brother's bullet-riddled truck, she pulled out her cell phone and called Jocelyn and then Deamber. After making both calls, she whispered to Balil, "Tell me what happened."

He began to tell her.

~ ~ ~

Jocelyn's biggest fear had come to pass. Something had happened to her son. India hadn't revealed too much, simply told her she needed to get to South Side Hospital. After waking her girls, Denean, and her grandson, they all jumped into Denean's truck. He had to be okay. He just had to be. Her faith in God wouldn't allow her to think otherwise.

Denean drove in silence, forcing herself to go the speed limit. Nothing serious was wrong with him. She'd reach the hospital and he'd get on her about worrying so much. He always told her she worried too much. Well, she couldn't stop herself. She loved him. She needed him. Their son and unborn child needed him. She gripped the steering wheel tightly.

They were supposed to get married on his sixteenth birthday. He promised he would never leave her and their children. People went to the hospital all the time. "He's fine," she said out loud. She believed that. Derrick Jr. began to cry. "I love you, sexy," she whispered.

~ ~ ~

India tried to prepare herself for what was coming her way. The call to Denean was less stressful, but she too was on her way, along with her brother and LaRon's right-hand man, who had been out with her brothers and had left moments before the shooting.

Jayson told India he was close by and he'd be at the hospital shortly. She needed all the support she could get. He arrived first, and after he talked to India, he entered the hospital with tears in his eyes, on his way to see his best friend. The city would be turned upside down once the two of them got done with it. Jay assured her that they'd find out who did it, and when they did, niggas would pay.

Denean came to a screeching halt and jumped out and attempted to run straight into the emergency room. Her eyes stared in horror at LaRon's truck.

India feared this reaction would come. She wished they had moved his damn truck, but knew why they didn't. Evidence technicians were already going through it. She wrapped Denean in a powerful embrace, preventing her from entering the hospital. "Denean, you have to remain calm. You're pregnant."

Denean didn't care. She didn't care about anything other

than being near the man she loved. She struggled mightily. "Get off me! Let me go! I got to go see him."

"He's gone." The words tore at her heart.

Jocelyn sat immobile in the front seat, afraid to get out. She saw the destroyed truck that belonged to her son's brother. The window was down enough for her to hear India's words: "He's gone." Had she said that? She couldn't have, but Denean was screaming. Screaming so loud she caused Mika, Chelle, and Lil D to start crying.

"He's gone," India repeated, her eyes locking onto Jocelyn's.

Screaming now herself, Jocelyn jumped out of the truck and tried to race into the hospital.

India only had two arms, and she needed them both. When Clyde Dexter, the cop, grabbed Jocelyn, she thanked him with her eyes. Balil came out and India told him to go get the kids out of the truck. Denean went limp in her arms. She began to talk softly to her.

Clyde had a difficult time trying to restrain the woman he held in his arms. He looked in India's direction hoping she came to assist him. He thought the woman tried to bite him several times. As he watched India whisper into the hysterical girl's ear, he saw that she began to calm down. He was glad when India made her way to him and hugged the woman he happily let go. Again, the whispered words. He still couldn't hear what was said.

After she got them both to calm down, she led them both into the hospital with her arms around their waists.

At the sight of Jocelyn and Denean, LaRon, who was getting stitches in his face, motioned the doctors away and started crying as he hugged them both.

"Can you all please leave out and give us a few minutes?" India asked.

Clyde had been waiting patiently to get some answers. He stood out in the hallway and was the one who shut the door to give the family some privacy. He had plenty of time to ask questions.

In the room with her were LaRon, Jayson, Jocelyn, and Denean. She stood close to them as her face hardened. "My baby brother is dead," she whispered. "The motherfuckers responsible for his death are out there. We are going to bury D, and then we are gonna find these niggas before the cops do. Am I understood?"

Everyone nodded.

The only one who had seen this side of India was LaRon. He knew a sleeping beast had been unleashed.

"Whoever these niggas is, is our business."

Outside the room, he didn't care that doctors and nurses saw him with his ear pressed up against the door, trying to hear what was being said in the room. He couldn't hear a word, but he did hear someone as they approached the door. He stepped back just as it began to open.

"Excuse me, Sergeant. More family is arriving," India told him. She could hear Deamber crying and screaming out in the waiting room. "I got to go comfort her."

He let her pass. He looked into the room and he saw the hardened glare from everyone still in the room. That's not what surprised him. That no one was crying anymore is what had him. Who the hell is this beautiful woman, he wondered to himself.

Before Derrick was removed from the hospital, India took everyone into the room they had his body in so they could have a moment alone with him. Denean's parents showed up, as well as two top members of LaRon's team. Denean was admitted into the hospital as a safety precaution with her blood pressure spiking so high. So, after LaRon was stitched up, India sent everyone home. She told Jocelyn that she'd handle all the paperwork.

Not only was Jocelyn not capable of much right then, but it gave India some much-needed time alone with her little brother. She locked the door, pulled a chair up beside his bed, and sat down. The blood was cleaned off his face, but the bullet hole looked like a third eye in the center of his forehead. A sheet covered his body, but his head was exposed. Tears now ran down her cheeks, controlled tears that didn't convulse her body, that went unheard. She cried for the death of her brother and for what she knew she had to do. It wouldn't be the first time she had to avenge one of her brothers. But she thought she'd never have to kill again.

~ ~ ~

Six Years Earlier

She knew something was wrong even before she put the key into the lock. Her mom's cousin Marcia was yelling, and her voice could be heard through the walls and doors. She hated that they had to stay with her, but it was better than being put away in a home. For the most part, she wasn't bad. At least she wasn't a crackhead. She did have a huge vice: men. India lost count on how many different men Marcia claimed as her man. And it didn't end there. The man would move into the already cramped five-bedroom Section 8 home. Besides her and her two brothers, Marcia had three kids as well. Before she could even learn his name, it would be over, and within a day or two another man would move in. The cycle was sad to India. What she tried to do is stay out of her cousin's way, and she totally ignored the men.

The men stared at her, but only one—the latest one—had crossed the line. He brushed his hand up against her butt, by accident he said. The same night, he entered the room she shared with her brothers. She woke up and saw him standing at the door smiling. She called him a pervert. He laughed and left. The next morning, she bought a straight razor. If he tried anything with her or her brothers, she'd kill him. She didn't know if she'd go through with it, but she'd be ready. She opened the door.

"If you had any weed, which I doubt, Russell wouldn't steal it."

LaRon was so upset he was crying. He was far from a crybaby, so India knew he was mad. What had him heated was India had told him it was his job to bring in the money. She'd given him all the work. Now it was gone.

India closed the door a little louder than she normally did, causing them to turn and look at her. She saw Balil standing silently in the doorway of the room they shared. "My brother doesn't lie. What's going on?"

Marcia was surprised by her arrival. Before she could stop herself, a nervous twitch began in her eyebrow, before traveling down to her shoulders. At first, she had no idea where the twitch came from, and then she realized it only appeared when India was around. Being twenty-nine, Marcia was fifteen years older than her little second cousin. She wasn't afraid of her; India was strange and made her nervous. "If he's not lying, is he holding drugs?"

"To pay for things we need and to give you a few dollars to help out," India answered.

Marcia understood the slight dig. Yeah, she spent the money she got from the checks she received from welfare. It wasn't nearly as much as she was promised by the caseworker, but it came in handy. Raising kids wasn't cheap. The times she got money from India, she assumed the girl got it from a boy. Her cuz was gorgeous, but from what she observed, she wasn't interested in boys. She often wondered if her little cousin was into girls?

India could tell her cousin was trying to come up with a lie. "Don't worry about it. It's gone now. There ain't nothing we can do about it." She took ahold of her brother's arm, led him to their room, and shut the door.

Marcia watched them go into the room. That girl is strange, she thought. She wondered why Russell had left out so quickly. She tried to call his thieving ass, but he didn't pick up.

In the bedroom, LaRon showed his sister the empty box where the weed once was. "He took it, India. I had a sale so I went to the stash and forgot to put it back. Me and Russell was the only two in the house. I came back to put the money away, and it was gone."

She wiped her brother's face. "Stop crying. I'll get it back." The two ounces was all they had. She wasn't taking that on the chin. One way or another, she was going to get her weed back from Russell.

"I want my weed back," she said as soon as the front door opened.

Seeing her standing at his door shocked Russell. He didn't know she knew where he lived. Damn, she was fine as hell. Put Marcia to shame in the looks department. He had brushed up against her young ass before and she hadn't said anything. He figured she liked it, but when he attempted to go in later that night, she called him a pervert. Now she was at his door. He smiled. "What weed?"

He could act stupid if he wanted; she'd play along for a minute. "The weed you stole out my room." She wasn't leaving without her weed.

Russell knew what body she hid under her coat. He had no idea how old she was, but she had a grown woman's body. This was his chance to find out if she knew how to work it. "Wanna come in?"

India stepped by him into his apartment. Instantly she smelled the aroma of weed—her weed. She wasn't nervous, nor afraid. Just wary.

Her ass could use a little fattening, but she knew how to move it. He licked his lips letting her know he was looking and he liked what he saw. He adjusted his dick as it got hard. "What are you willing to do to get it back, if I did have it?" By now he had locked his front door and was standing near her. Standing right up on her he thought his size would intimidate her. She neither flinched nor backed up. She just stared at him. Taking her silence as agreement, he zipped down her zipper on her coat. He pushed her coat open, exposing the T-shirt that covered her breasts. He ran his hand over the fabric, pinching her nipples.

India pushed his hand away. "I want my weed."

Russell palmed her ass and pulled her toward him, grinding into her as he did. "You want your weed and I want some of this young, tight pussy. Fair exchange ain't no robbery." He rubbed her crotch through her jeans.

He had her mistaken. She shoved him hard enough to cause him to stumble backward. A lamp crashed to the floor as Russell knocked it over.

"Bitch!" he hissed. He recovered quickly, and as he did, he backhanded India, sending her to the floor. He snatched her up by her jacket and tossed her onto the couch. "You gonna give me some pussy, bitch." He took out his dick and began to stroke it.

India rolled over onto her side, reached into her pocket and came into contact with her switchblade.

"So you like it doggy." He rubbed her ass, squeezed it, and smacked it.

"Lay down," she whispered softly.

His hand rested on her ass. "Huh?"

"Lay down. I want to be on top."

He couldn't believe it. He wasn't a rapist, but he was ready to take her young pussy. He started removing his clothes as he talked. "I'll give you all your weed back, lil mami I'll give you some money too. Let me take care of you from now on."

There was no way she could overpower him. He was much stronger and bigger. She got up and looked down at him—completely naked, his dick standing straight up. It was the first time in her thirteen years she had seen a naked man outside of a school book. With his eyes on her, she took off all of her clothes and walked to sit them on a chair.

He watched her every move, trembling with anticipation. He was dropping Marcia's ass and making India wifey. When she straddled his waist and took his dick into her left hand, positioning his dick at her opening, he closed his eyes. He knew her pussy was going to be the best ever.

"Click."

The sound was unmistakable. His eyes shot open, but he didn't dare move. The blade she held at his throat bit into his skin. He looked at her face. There was no look of desire—only hate tinged with rage. "Please don't kill me. I'll give you back your weed and all my money."

"Too late," she whispered. With one quick slice, she opened his throat from ear to ear. Blood shot out, hitting her on her naked body. India stood up and watched Russell clutch at his throat and thrash on the floor. She didn't kill him because he took her weed.Not even for hitting her and calling her a bitch. No, he was dying because he tried to do it to her knowing she was a kid. If he tried it with her, he'd try it with another kid. Now he didn't have that option. His thrashing stopped and he took his last breath. He was dead.

After getting into his shower, she located her weed and the couple of hundred dollars he had. Once she was dressed, she used a pile of his clothes to start a fire on top of his body. She waited until a nice fire was started before she left out and returned to her home.

"I got our weed back. Make sure you don't lose it again," she told her brother.

Nothing else was said about it.

~ ~ ~

Present Day

As she wiped tears from her face, she leaned down and kissed Derrick softly on his lips. "I love you, lil Bro. I'll get them. That's a promise." As she exited his room, she locked eyes with the cop.

"I waited around for you," Jayson informed her.

He was like a brother to her. She hugged him. "Go to LaRon. I got to stay here a little while, and then I'm staying with Denean," she explained. With her brother's girl being admitted, she wanted her to know that no matter what, she'd always be family.

Jayson left. Before signing the paperwork, she called Jocelyn, making sure she got home. Clyde watched her get on the elevator. She was a special woman. He finally left.

He still had a lot of paperwork to do. As he rode away, an ambulance was pulling in with another shooting victim.

F IFTEEN

She didn't leave the hospital until close to noon. After returning home and showering, she called LaRon and told him she needed $50,000 in cash. He was to have it ready by the time she got to his home in Forest Hills. India had to get some answers, and she knew where to start.

LaRon wasn't trying to hear nothing Deamber had to say when it came to her voicing her fears and worries about his health and safety. Derrick was dead, and he didn't think he'd ever sleep right until he killed the niggas responsible.

This was even a time when India couldn't tell him shit. He blamed himself for his brother getting killed. He didn't recognize the niggas that tried to get at them, but he figured they were trying to rob them. That's all it could've been. With his sis calling him and telling him she needed fifty stacks, he knew she was up to something. She hadn't said anything more, but she didn't have to. Whatever she was up to, he wanted in. He was in and he didn't care who didn't like it. By the time India reached him, he was dressed and ready to go. He didn't even let India get out of her car. He kissed Deamber and left out.

India saw the look on her brother's face and knew it would be a waste of time telling him to do as the doctor ordered and rest. "Your ass looks like Frankenstein with them stitches," she joked.

LaRon smiled as she pulled out of his driveway. He was glad she didn't attempt to tell him he couldn't go along with her. "What's up?"

They knew each other so well. "Denean is getting out of

the hospital later this afternoon. Her parents are with her, but I sent Balil over there. She's gonna need us."

He'd thought of her as well. He was going to make sure she was straight, her and the babies. "She's family."

India nodded. They rode in silence for a few minutes.

"Sis, I got my people on this. Why don't you let me handle this?"

"I'm the oldest and it's my job. Told you when Mom died that I'd take care of y'all. Ain't shit change. My baby brother is dead. Niggas gonna pay for killing him."

He agreed with that. "I don't want anything to happen to you, that's all."

"Trust your sis can take care of herself."

He didn't doubt that. Even prior to their mom dying, she took care of herself and them. He never told her he knew she killed Russell, but now he said, "You proved that with Russell."

She smiled but said nothing. She thought he figured it all out after news spread of Russell's death. At first everyone thought he died in a fire. Homicide detectives came around and it was revealed his throat getting slashed was the real cause of his death. She noticed the way LaRon looked at her when they came to the house to talk to Marcia since she was the last person Russell talked to. She'd left numerous nasty messages on his cell phone after he stole the weed—one threatening him with death. Of course, after awhile, interest in the case died down and it went unsolved.

"Do you know who owns Rock Jungle?"

He only met the owner because of the party he had there for Derrick. He was an Italian by the name of Mike Astari. He got the number because India was turning 21 on November 9. He planned on having her surprise party there. "Yeah. Why?"

"Call him and see if he can meet us."

He wanted to ask her more, but he took out his phone and scrolled to the name he just put in there the day before. He pushed Send.

"Hello."

"Hey, Mike. This is the young guy that had the party at your club last night."

Mike sat at his dining room table sipping a cup of coffee, eating an apple danish, and reading the newspaper. "LaRon, my condolences on the death of your brother."

He thought the man would have trouble remembering him, but he obviously hadn't. "Thank you. Do you think I can see you?"

He had no clue what this call was about, and normally he wouldn't have considered it. The only reason he did is because the kid lost his little brother and it was at his place. The article in the paper he was reading already shed a negative light on his club. Mike was on damage control. Besides, he had good instincts. "Sure. When?"

LaRon mouthed the word "when" to his sister and she mouthed "ASAP." "Now, if you can manage it."

He looked at his watch. He had to meet a detective handling the investigation at three o'clock. It was nearing two. He had a few minutes to spare. "I'll be at Rock Jungle in fifteen minutes. You can meet me there."

"He's meeting us at his club now," LaRon told his sister after he hung up. "Why are we going to see him?" He still didn't get it.

India use to go to the Jungle, using a fake ID, when she was fifteen and sixteen. She remembered all the cameras around the club and inside of it. One of them had to have captured the shootout. "The cameras had to see everything. I want to see the two niggas that killed D. I want you to hit the streets with their photo and find out where they lay their heads. We got to move on this fast because the jakes are gonna want that footage too, if they ain't already got it."

Now he got it. LaRon would never forget what either of the niggas looked like.

But if he circulated their photos, more people would know. Jayson would make that happen.

It took Michael Astari mere minutes to realize two major things after sitting across a table from LaRon and his sister India: (1) The men responsible for killing their brother were walking dead men, and (2) India was a calculating, deadly woman who also happened to be the most beautiful and stunning woman he'd seen in his forty-two years of living. "I have an appointment with a cop at three, so you caught me before I turned anything over to them," he said after hearing what they wanted. He stood up. "Give me a minute."

Sitting in the club area evoked painful memories for them both. This was the last place their brother had enjoyed himself. They sat in silence deep in thought.

Mike returned with a disk. "This is the original and only copy of the incident, so don't lose it. Take it, and I hope it helps."

India dug into her purse and took out the fifty stacks LaRon had just given her. "Thank you so much, Mike."

He smiled. He liked the woman's style. If he wasn't afraid of catching a bullet, he would ask her to drop her pants so he could see if she had the right set of equipment. The lady had balls of steel and ice running through her veins. "No charge," he said as he stared into her eyes. "If the time ever comes when you need my help, I don't want you to hesitate."

They got to their feet and both shook his hand. The doorbell sounded.

"That's probably the cop," he announced. He saw their look. "I take it y'all don't want them to see you. Go out the back."

"Thanks again," India said. She put the money back into her purse and followed her brother out the back door.

After waiting for the door to close, Mike went to the front door and opened it. "Sorry to keep you gentlemen waiting. Come in."

He acted like was listening intently. He nodded at all the appropriate times, just waiting for the request. When it came, he went off to get it. "We have a problem," he said when he returned from going off after the surveillance tape. "It's blank. My manager must not have started it last night," he lied smoothly. He did turn over the tapes from inside the club. He doubted that would be of any help. "I'm sorry I couldn't be more helpful," he said at the front door. "If I hear anything, I'll call you."

"Thanks for your time, Mr. Astari," Clyde Dexter said. He went along with his good friend Maurice Holt, a homicide detective, because he thought they'd at least see the faces of the killer(s).

After locking the door, Mike went into his office and picked up his office phone, punched in ten digits and waited. It was picked up on the third ring. "I'm about to fax you two photos of two men. Pretty sure they'll have a record. I want to know everything about them."

"I'll do what I can," the woman on the other end promised.

Mike hung up, confident that she'd get it done. Tessa Brentwood worked in the downtown FBI. building. Whenever he needed her, she always came through. Over the years, during his climb in the mafia, Mike kept Tessa in his pocket. Now that he was head of the Pittsburgh mob, he had connections to get the answers he searched for. And when he got them, he'd turn them over to India Jones. He looked forward to seeing her again.

India left South Side and headed straight home. There were a lot of things she had to do: contact a funeral director, check on Jocelyn, the girls, Denean, and her nephew, but first thing she had to do was see the faces of the niggas responsible for killing Derrick. The CD-ROM Mike had given her would reveal them.

As soon as she got in her home, she put it in the DVD player and sat down next to her brother.

LaRon stared at the screen. "This is where D knocks one nigga out."

The punch was in actual time. Mike had excellent cameras, because everything was clear. LaRon watched as Derrick hit the nigga to the ground. Then the three brothers started walking away, until they disappeared from view.

This is the part he hadn't seen, what the guys did after they walked away. "Balil took their guns. One must've had another on him."

India was waiting for one of them to pull another gun out. People began to hurry past the two men. And then one man stopped right in front of them. There was no audio on the CD, but from his movements, India could tell he was upset.

LaRon stood up. He couldn't believe what he was seeing. But there was no way his eyes were deceiving him.

As the man turned just as a gun was tossed down, India was able to see his face. She looked over at her brother. Tears fell from his eyes. The man stood by as one of the other men picked the gun up, raised it, and began to fire. They both knew what he was shooting at. All three men began to run.

Not only was the third man well-known to India and LaRon, but he was also close to them—so much so that seeing him on the TV screen in the act wasn't enough to convince them it was real. They had to talk to him. In their heart the both knew it was as it appeared.

Jayson, LaRon's right hand and his baby mom's older brother was the man.

LaRon had thought it was just a random robbery attempt. Finding out Jayson was involved put a whole other spin on things. He'd been in the house out Altoona, knew every single stash spot he had. As it all came together, he knew it wasn't a robbery attempt. No—it was a hit. And the target was supposed to be him. Jayson tried to kill him. That knowledge had him fucked up. The nigga was just in the hospital crying and vowing revenge on those responsible for killing D. All along, he was behind it. The slimy-ass nigga was dead. LaRon wasn't thinking straight and reached for his phone, intending on calling Jayson and telling him he was dead on sight.

India took the phone from him. "His day is going to come. Right now we act like we don't know he was in on it." Her brother didn't agree, but she had her reason for doing it this way. Jayson and LaRon were like brothers. But closer than their relationship was Jayson and Deamber's relationship. She wanted to see if the deceit ran deeper. If it did, she'd get rid of them both.

After dropping off LaRon, she called White's Funeral Home. She'd bury her brother like a star and then kill all those responsible.

Sixteen

The death of her son sent Jocelyn into a deep state of shock and depression. She heard India and knew whoever was responsible would ultimately pay with their lives. Yet that brought her little solace. No matter what pain the niggas endured, Derrick would still be dead. She'd never see his smile, hear his laugh, or feel his strong arms hug her. They'd talked about his goals and dreams. He wanted to do something with his life—to help make things better in Garfield. Now he'd never get to do any of that.

Locating his siblings was the best thing to happen to him. He was so happy. A bullet ended it all on his fifteenth birthday. Why? Why had God allowed him to die? After years of drug use and disbelief and indifference, Jocelyn's faith in God had slowly begun to return. She now wanted to join her son in death. Living, she reasoned, only brought heartache and sorrow. In the days following his murder, Jocelyn secluded herself in her room, contemplating suicide. She didn't want to talk, eat, or hear how much Derrick wouldn't want her to give up. She'd given up. She was just a coward. Help came from an unlikely source on a day when she thought she couldn't go on another day.

"Jocelyn?"

With the lights off, Jocelyn lay on her bed. In her hands, gripped tightly, was a bottle of sleeping pills. She had no idea what the name of the pills was. She bought them from a woman for fifty dollars. All she knew was if she took enough of them, she'd never wake up again. Painless, but final. Hearing her name, she opened her eyes.

Michelle stepped further into the room. It wasn't too long ago that she was in a similar position—wanting time to stop, to rewind and go back to before her child was killed. She knew what Jocelyn was going through. Crack was her crutch. She tried to drown her pain and sorrow in its use. She would still be getting high if she hadn't had the dream, a dream so vivid that even after awakening, the happiness remained. When she got the news that Derrick was dead, Michelle lost all hope. If it wasn't for Derrick, she would have been dead awhile ago. He refused to give up on her. She cried so much that she cried herself to sleep. That's when the dream came.

Recognizing her voice, Jocelyn asked, "Did you want to die after your child was killed?"

Michelle could hear the despair in Jocelyn's voice, could tell that she was crying. Michelle sat down on the bed and took one of Jocelyn's hands into both her own. "Every single day since she's been gone. I've smoked so much crack since then that I hoped it induced a heart attack. Having to bury my daughter is the hardest thing I've ever had to do."

Jocelyn didn't want to live that long, didn't want to see her son put into the ground. Just the thought of it sent dread throughout her body. "I want to die."

Tears began to fall down Michelle's face. In her dream, Derrick came to her. "He's in a better place," she whispered. "A place where there is no more death. No guns, crack, gangs, sadness or pain—just pure joy and happiness."

Her words angered Jocelyn. Fuck heaven. She wanted to scream. "There ain't no God and ain't no heaven. If he was real, why does he let this type of thing happen?"

The tears were running freely now, but Michelle smiled through them. "Derrick told me you'd say that."

This bitch done smoked too much crack, Jocelyn thought. She was crazy. Michelle knew what Jocelyn was thinking. If the shoe was on the other foot and Jocelyn had come to her telling her Kelly had talked to her in a dream, she would have thought she was crazy. But she wasn't crazy. "He came to me, Jocelyn. He came to talk to me. Me." She still had trouble believing it. "He told me to tell you that he is fine. He said he loves you and that Nana Rose was at the gate waiting on him."

A chill ran through Jocelyn's body as soon as she heard the name. Jocelyn was just eight years old when her grandmother died. There was no way Michelle could have known about her nana. She wanted to believe her so much.

"Kelly is fine. He saw her, hugged her, and she told him to tell me she loves me. Joc, you don't know how much I needed to hear that. Our kids are together in heaven."

Jocelyn was crying tears of happiness. She loved her nana, and Derrick was in heaven, alongside Jesus. The two women cried as they hugged. A heavy burden was lifted from both of them.

Michelle stayed with Jocelyn awhile longer and they prayed before she returned to her home. At home, Michelle went up to her room and cleaned up and tossed out all the crack she had. Never again would she smoke crack.

Since the birth of her son, Denean and her parents' broken relationship began to repair. After Derrick's death, she leaned heavily on them. She didn't know how she'd go on without him, how she'd raise not one but two small children on her own. She really didn't want to see her son. He reminded her too much of his father. The prospect of living a life without Derrick didn't seem like much of a life. Junior was barred from her room and her parents took care of him. She couldn't bring herself to sleep in the room she shared with Derrick, so she moved back in with her parents. No one seemed to get it.

She didn't want to eat, didn't want to live; all she wanted is her Sexy back. She'd never hear him call her "Gorgeous" again.

"Hey, Sista," India said as she entered Denean's room.

She was sitting on her bed, looking in one of her many photo albums, a smile etched across her face as she looked at pictures they took at Sandcastle. His trunks came off at one point as he exited the water. Denean never laughed so hard. As the saying goes, he who laughs last, laughs the hardest. He had handed her eight pieces of paper with numbers on them from different women—one even going as far as writing she wouldn't mind a threesome with Denean. "She's right," the note ended. Denean was disgusted. Of course she destroyed them. They had so many good times. There were so many memories. Now he was gone. Seeing India, who was the female version of Derrick, wasn't something she wanted right then. She'd been avoiding her and LaRon because of how similar they all looked. "Hey," she greeted weakly. She closed the photo album.

India smiled brightly as she hugged and kissed Denean. She went to the window and opened it. "Girl, it's beautiful out. October and sunny. You sitting up in your room, hair all twisted."

The comment drew a smile from Denean and she played with her hair a second before giving up. She knew India was trying to make her feel better. She knew the day would come when she'd go on living. This day wasn't it.

"My neph's downstairs looking adorable. Want me to go get him?" She knew from her parents that Denean hadn't seen her son in days and she didn't want any company.

"No."

India sat on the bed and rubbed Denean's stomach. She was at a loss for words.

"My baby will never meet his or her father." Tears began to fall. "We didn't go to find out what we were having. He said it didn't matter. He was more than my children's father. He was my best friend. What am I going to do without him?"

That was a question India couldn't answer. She hugged her again. "You have to eat. You're eating for two. Derrick wouldn't want you laying up here like this. He's gone, baby. It hurts. You got his son and hopefully his daughter to raise. You got to tell them who their father was. Let them know how much he loved them."

She knew everything India said was true. She couldn't bring herself to do anything but cry. Soon she was asleep, dreaming of Derrick.

India left her. She had the final plans for the funeral to handle.

~ ~ ~

It was chilly the day of Derrick's funeral, but that didn't stop anyone from showing up. Well over a thousand people showed up. Word had gotten out that maybe it was some niggas from Homewood who killed him and some form of retaliation was supposed to jump off. LaRon quickly spread word that if anyone disrespected his brother's funeral, they would be dealt with.

A lot of his team was seeing him for the first time. LaRon kept a low profile. Jayson was the one seen, the one many thought ran shit.

"Remember what I said," India whispered to him as soon as she looked up and saw Jayson making his way toward them.

He hadn't seen or talked to Jayson since he found out about his deception. He wanted to pull his gun from under his arm and kill the nigga right then. He had the nerve to be crying. If Jayson walked up on him and attempted to touch him, LaRon would snap.

India saw the look in her brother's eyes. She left his side

and intercepted Jayson before it got out of control. She said something to him and hugged him. They talked for a minute, and then Jayson turned away.

LaRon couldn't believe the nigga showed up at the funeral. His days were numbered.

Denean sat with her head on her friend Mutter's shoulder. She refused to look in the direction of the casket. Her depression ran deep, and India knew she'd need the support of all the family and friends that loved her. She rubbed Denean's back and touched Mutter's hand.

Balil had a tough time dealing with his brother's death. He sat all the way in the back between Tamika and Rachelle. He stood up and hugged her. He was another that didn't want to approach the casket.

Many in the room felt that way. India accepted hugs and condolences from complete strangers. Her brother was well-liked and respected. As she squatted and hugged Tamika, she looked up and saw the three cops as they entered the room. She locked eyes with the one in the middle, Clyde Dexter. She stood up.

Everyone turned and looked at the cops. India waited for the three men to make their way over to where she stood. She hoped they weren't coming to arrest Jayson. As of yet, she hadn't received word on the other two she wanted. It really didn't matter. She planned on approaching Jayson soon; he'd provide their names and whereabouts after she got through with him. "Why are you here?" She noticed Jayson moving closer to the side door. She hoped he got away if they came to arrest him. His ass was hers.

Clyde had thought of her often in the five days since he first laid eyes on her. When he thought of the big investigation he was heading, he had no clue he'd once again be crossing her path. Right then he had men outside taking down every license plate of all those entering the funeral home. He turned and looked at the kid he met at the hospital with glass in his face— the head of his investigation, the brother of the woman he couldn't stop thinking about. He didn't know much about LaRon Jones or India Jones. He hated that he had to do it, but he had a job to do. He hoped she didn't have anything to do with her brother's drug enterprise. "My condolences once again on the death of your brother, Ms. Jones. I'm here on official business. My boss ordered me to take down all the license plates of everyone attending this funeral." He held out the order.

India ignored the paper he held out for her to look at if she wanted. "There are no vehicles in here, so please take your men and get the hell out."

He guessed he deserved that. He motioned for the two officers to go before him and followed them out.

Watching him go, she wondered what their wanting to get all the plates was all about. She figured a lot of the men in attendance were drug dealers, but why inform them? An investigation was being conducted. On who, was what had her perplexed. It was time for her to have a talk with LaRon. She wasn't going to lose another brother to prison or a grave.

India stood by as people came up to speak about her brother. A lot of the young guys could not get through their speech, and it was India who hugged them and told them it was going to be okay.

The line of cars stretched close to a mile. People that didn't know who was being buried assumed from all the cars, and cop escort, that someone famous was being buried. He was loved by many, but was killed at just fifteen years old.

At the gravesite, Michelle's rendition of "Amazing Grace" brought everyone to tears. As dirt was being thrown onto her brother's casket, India's face hardened and she turned to

LaRon.

"It's time," she said as she hugged him.

LaRon cut his eyes and looked at Jayson, who was still crying. He had his arm around Denean. The time was near and he'd avenge his brother's death.

As they all began to leave, India got a call from Michael Astari. "I got something you might want to see."

She hung up. The plan was to get Jayson up to the home in Altoona. There he'd reveal the other two names, and then his life would end. She told LaRon she had to do something and left.

At Rock Jungle, India watched the footage that Mike had for her, in disbelief.

"I recognized them from the video I had of them from the night your brother was killed. I own the restaurant they were eating at and I happened to be in there."

She couldn't believe what she was seeing. It couldn't be what she was thinking. It just couldn't. Yet she saw it with her own eyes. She thanked Mike, and while she sat in her car, she called LaRon with tears in her eyes. "Bring Deamber," she said.

The fourth person at the restaurant along with Jayson and the two niggas that tried to rob/kill her brothers was Deamber. What part she played in all this, they'd soon find out. She loved Deamber and she was pregnant with LaRon's second child. If she had her hand in Derrick getting killed, she would face the same fate as her brother—both would die.

SEVENTEEN

The property that LaRon owned in Altoona was both spacious and secluded. It sat on four acres of land and was the perfect place for what India had planned. She wasn't sure if either Jayson or Deamber would cooperate, and in the event that they didn't, it would not only get messy, but extremely loud. The fact that she was just hours away from killing again didn't bother her—not if they were guilty, and Jayson definitely was.

She hoped there was a reason Deamber had for sitting amongst her brother's killers. She couldn't see why either of them would want LaRon dead. It would be a question she'd ask them.

India arrived hours earlier than anyone. It wasn't long before a truck, driven by an old black man, pulled up out front in the driveway. She went out and shook his hand.

"You get more and more gorgeous every time I see you, Miss Lady."

"Go ahead, Mr. Gary, before I tell your wife you be out here flirting."

He slammed the truck door and smiled. "Where do you want me to set up?"

India knew Mr. Gary from her brother's dealings with him. Gary Townsend bred and trained pit bulls. It was reported that there was no better trainer in the city, maybe in the state. India hoped it was true. She wanted those responsible to suffer greatly for killing her brother. She stepped back as he opened the back and six pits jumped out onto the ground and then stood obediently at his side—all of them eyeing her.

"You're fine. They only attack when I give the command. Would you like a demonstration?"

That's the last thing she wanted, and who did he expect them to demonstrate on? Her? "No thanks. Follow me."

She hadn't told anyone her plan—not even Mr. Gary. She told him where to leave the dogs, the indoor racquetball court, and had him move his truck around back out of sight. She looked at her watch. They'd be there shortly.

LaRon wanted to keep Deamber out of it. He knew how close she was to her brother. Jayson was dead. As much as he loved the nigga, he did not have much time to live. There was no way he could allow him to live. LaRon just wanted to know one thing, why? Why was he a part of a plan to kill him? He still didn't know why his sister wanted Deamber there, but he'd do it just as India told him to do.

"Why can't I wait and ride with you or drive up there myself?" Deamber asked LaRon.

"Stop asking so many questions. I ain't got no clue who these niggas is. They still might be tryin' to get at me. I want Jay to take you so you got some protection."

Sounded logical to her, but Deamber wanted LaRon at her side. She loved him. "How long is it going to take for you to get up there?"

He hugged her. "Not too much later than it'll take y'all to get there."

"Okay, baby." She kissed him and they made love on the living room floor. Panting and exhausted, she licked his sweaty neck. "I love you, LaRon."

"Love you too," he said and meant it. He had no idea how much that love would be tested in a little while.

The only thing she told LaRon was that Jay would talk. As he walked into his house in Altoona, LaRon was on edge. He wanted Jay dead. LaRon left before Jay arrived to drive

Deamber up. He didn't trust himself to be around the nigga. Since finding out Jay tried to kill him, LaRon began to wonder who else in his click harbored those same feelings. Jay was like his brother. If he'd snake him, who could he trust? He hoped his sister could get Jay to talk. He wanted the other niggas involved and wouldn't be satisfied until Jay talked. "They're on their way."

"Park your shit out back. Initially I want you hidden when they come," she explained.

He had an opportunity to talk now. "Why you want Deamber here?" She nearly fainted at the sight of blood on TV. There was no way she could stand by and watch her brother be killed.

India had no intention of revealing Deamber's suspected involvement. Not now. LaRon was already too emotionally attached.

"Move your car."

He didn't see why she wanted her there, but he left out. India was up to something, and the fact he didn't know what had him nervous. Before he had a chance to question her further when he returned from moving his car, they both saw Jayson's Jaguar as he turned in to the long driveway.

"Go upstairs and hide until I call you." She walked to the door, looked over her shoulder to make sure LaRon was out of sight, and opened it, just as Deamber and Jayson got out of the car. She smiled.

"Where is LaRon?"

Deamber took her time but hugged India when she reached her.

"He had to handle something, but he'll be here."

"Hey, sis," Jay greeted her.

India allowed him to hug her. "Hey."

Always hungry, Deamber immediately smelled the aroma

of food in the distance. "What you cook?"

India laughed. "A little something." When she hugged Jayson, she felt the gun he had in its holster under his arm. "Jay, get comfortable. Dee, you can help me with the meal."

"I got niggas out on the block hunting the niggas responsible for spanking Lil D down," Jay called out from the living room. He turned on the PlayStation intending on playing Madden, and sat down. "It ain't gonna be long."

India poured dressing into the caesar salad as she stood at the counter. "We're close to catching them," she announced loud enough for Jay to hear her.

He sat the wireless remote down as he got to his feet. This was news to him.

Marley and a nigga named Trigger were holed up in a hotel, waiting on the next opportunity to finish what they came from Detroit to do: kill LaRon. That Derrick was killed was unfortunate, but that didn't stop his plan. And that plan was to become the boss. On some real shit, he was the boss already. He made all the deliveries, handled all disputes, put in the footwork, and distributed all the money. All LaRon did is stack money off all his blood and sweat.

The plan was formulated on a trip he took to meet a ring model he met in Vegas at the Roy Jones vs. Bernard Hopkins fight. She lived in Detroit. It was there he met up with Marley, Candy's brother. One night, Marley told him how much dope was popping in the city, but how there was none in the city. Jay told LaRon about it, thinking it could bring in more money, but he barely listened to him before telling him no. He didn't even give

him the decency to hear him out. Simply no. Jay felt like a damn flunky. He realized he'd have to handle things as the mafia handles things: kill the Don. LaRon was the don and had to go. If the two niggas hadn't fucked up, he could have already taken over. The transition would be very easy and smooth. All he had to do is wait for the right time to, and then kill LaRon. He should have done it himself all along. No one would have suspected him. Originally, he had a problem with killing his best friend.

He stepped in the doorway leading to the kitchen, knowing that LaRon's end was near and it would probably have to be by his hands. He had no idea what India meant about being close to catching the niggas. LaRon hadn't said anything. "Y'all heard something?"

India knew Jay was a killer, and with him having his gun on him, she'd have to get the upper hand on him. She opened up a cupboard door, acting like she was reaching for some type of seasoning, but instead grabbed the .380 she hid there. Turning, she pointed it at him. "Yeah, we heard you is a slimy bitch-ass, nigga!"

Jayson heard her words in disbelief. How did they know? He didn't give it another moment's thought. He jumped out of the way just as India pulled the trigger. The bullet slammed into the wall harmlessly.

India realized her mistake. Allowing too much distance between her and Jay. Deamber was within arm's distance, and India quickly snatched her up, using her as a shield.

Jayson had his gun in his hand. He peeked around the corner and saw India holding a gun to his trembling and terrified sister's head. "India, it's not what you think."

India pulled Deamber behind the large stainless-steel refrigerator. "Oh, isn't it?"

Deamber had no idea what was going on. That Jayson and India were about to have a gun battle blew her mind.

There was no way Jay was going to put his sister in jeopardy. He thought he might be able to sneak around back and get the drop on her. Just as he was about to turn around, he felt the hard, cold steel press on the area right below his ear. "You pulled a strap on my sis, nigga."

Jay dropped his gun to the floor. "Bro, what's going on?"

Just hearing the word "bro" ate at LaRon. Jay wasn't any brother of his. The nigga trembling in front of him killed his real bro. He smashed the barrel of his nine into the side of Jay's face, opening a large gash and sending him crumbling to the floor. "Sis, you cool?" He heard the gunshot and didn't know who busted their gun.

India heard the exchange between her brother and Jayson and heard the sound of steel against bone. She walked out of the kitchen, holding Deamber's arm with her gun pointed in her back.

LaRon knew immediately that something was wrong. He could tell from the look on his woman's face. He had begun to wonder if Deamber knew of her brother's plan to kill him. The two were extremely close. The fight they'd gotten into about three weeks ago after she found out he cheated, flashed in his mind. She acted like she was over it, but obviously she wasn't. The fact she wanted him dead hurt more than anything.

Having no idea what was going on, Deamber looked into the eyes of the man she loved and trusted. "LaRon, please." She clutched her stomach. Right before India pushed her out of the kitchen, India said, "You better not had anything to do with my brother's death." It didn't register until she saw her brother on the floor unconscious.

"What's going on?"

LaRon ignored his woman as he reached down and pocketed Jay's gun.

"Take him to the handball room and leave him," India said.

The Plexiglass was four inches thick and virtually unbreakable. Besides, if he woke up any time soon, she doubted he'd move much with the pits eyeing him. LaRon began to drag Jay away, and she turned her attention to Deamber. She loved the girl, loved her like a sister. She still didn't understand why Deamber or Jay would want LaRon killed, but they obviously did. All she knew is Deamber sat at a table with three niggas who killed her brother. Guilt by association. Once she showed LaRon the video and they heard Deamber's excuse, she'd leave it up to LaRon to decide her fate. "Your fate is in LaRon's hands. Sit down," she instructed once they reached the couch.

Crying uncontrollably, she did as she was told. They couldn't think she had anything to do with Derrick being killed? Why had LaRon hit her brother? He didn't have anything to do with Derrick's death. She had no idea what was going on. Their families were one. Nothing but love between them. She watched LaRon enter the room, with pleading eyes.

"What's good?" he said, directing the question toward his sister.

"Mike contacted me and showed me something you might want to see." She inserted the CD into the Station, picked up the controller, and pushed play. It started to play.

Deamber watched the TV as well. When she saw what it was, she still didn't understand. Jay had met up with two dudes he knew from out of town. The only reason she'd been along with him is because her car had been vandalized and Jay had been nearby so had snatched her up. But what did any of that have to do with—

"Them are the two niggas that killed D. They must've been planning it right there."

"That's a lie!" Deamber screamed. Why was India lying? She vomited all over herself and onto the floor.

He wanted to go to her, to wipe up the vomit, but stopped himself from doing it. "Who is the two niggas you ate with?"

She had no idea who they were, her brother's friends from

out of town. "What?"

That she had something to do with the plot to kill him and his brother's death, hurt him deep. "Listen to me good, Deamber. Jay is as good as dead. Tell me you ain't plot with him to get me." He needed her answer. If she did have anything to do with the plot to kill him, he didn't know what he'd do.

"Kill you?" This was more than she could fathom. Kill him? She could never do him harm. Didn't he know that? They'd been together since they were both fourteen. She caught him cheating twice. Oh, she wanted to kill him, but couldn't. "LaRon, I love you more than life itself. If my brother had anything to do with plotting to harm you or for killing Derrick, I had nothing to do with it." She said all this while staring into his eyes, as tears ran down his cheeks.

India kept her eyes on Deamber the entire time. She believed her. Her instinct told her all she needed to know. Without saying a word, she walked by her brother and took Deamber into her arms. "I believe you."

Her relief was instant. She fell into India and just cried. She cried out of relief and because of her brother's fate. She knew he would soon be dead. She loved her brother. "Are y'all sure he had something to do with Derrick being killed?" She didn't have to mention that they thought she had something to do with it, when she didn't. They might be mistaken about Jayson too.

India switched CDs and allowed Deamber to watch the footage of the night Derrick was killed. There was no doubt that Jay was in on it. What she couldn't understand is why. LaRon loved her brother. She thought Jayson loved LaRon in return.

Whatever LaRon had, Jayson was more than welcome to. She lifted her head. "Please don't make him suffer," she pleaded.

That would be up to Jayson, India thought. One way or

another, she'd get the answers she was searching for. "Take her to get cleaned up and have her lay down."

LaRon did as he was told.

India headed toward the handball court. Jayson was sitting up, a dazed expression on his face, trying to be as still as possible.

"He got up a minute ago. Told him not to attempt to get up," Mr. Gary explained. "So far, he's listening."

With six pits surrounding him, India didn't blame him. "I'm going to ask him an important question. If he doesn't answer it . . ."

"You want my babies to encourage him a little?"

"Exactly." She didn't know what that entailed, but she didn't think Jayson would hold out too long. She opened the door and followed Mr. Gary in.

"India, please," he begged.

"Why, Jay? You're family."

He began to sob loudly, causing the dogs to stand and growl menacingly. He had fucked up. Fucked up bad. He saw no way out of it. He was dead and he knew it. He wasn't going to answer her. She wouldn't understand. It was a part of the game. He gambled and lost. "Are you going to kill me?"

Before India could answer him, LaRon stepped into the room. He overheard the question. "Yeah." He tossed Jay's cell phone into his lap. "I want the other two niggas. Where they at?"

If giving the niggas up meant saving his own life, he would have done it easily.

But he was getting nothing out of it. "Kill me."

India intended on asking him the same thing. She nodded to Mr. Gary. "Down!" he ordered.

The swiftness in which the dogs executed the command caught Jayson by surprise and made LaRon and India jump back. Within a few seconds, Jayson was flat on his back. A pit bull was locked on this throat, the dog's saliva dripping onto his neck. He shit himself.

"Don't struggle, son," Mr. Gary cautioned. He motioned for India, who came up to stand beside him. "Ask him anything you want. I think he'll answer now."

"Are you going to call them?" she asked.

There was no way he could answer. Breathing was proving difficult. The dog released its grip and he immediately raised his hand to his throat. It was bleeding and painful, but he sat up. After looking at the dogs, all of whom looked like they were going to attack, he picked up his cell phone.

"Tell them you are going to send a car for them," India told him.

He did as he was told and then hung up. "They're at the Holiday Inn in Wilkinsburg."

India called the limo she had on standby and told him where to go.

"Why, Jay?" LaRon asked him.

Jayson smiled up at them both and then answered LaRon's question. "You know why."

LaRon did know. Greed. Wanting to be top dawg. LaRon shook his head from side to side sadly. He intended on getting out of the game and turning the connect and his team over to Jayson. It was all going to be his. He didn't have to try to take it. Tears fell from his eyes.

"Sorry, bro."

"Me too," LaRon told him as he shot him in the center of his chest, killing him instantly.

The two were extremely close. She knew how hard this was for her brother. "Go. I'll clean this up."

LaRon left and returned to the room Deamber was in. She was out of the shower. They comforted each other, mourning the death of a man they both loved.

India shed tears over Jayson's death as well. She had loved him like he was one of her brothers. Now two brothers were gone because of drugs. She'd have a talk with LaRon real soon. He had to get out. She removed Jayson's body and then waited on the call from the driver she hired to pick up the two niggas destined for death.

EIGHTEEN

Marley Jacobs was the actual killer of Derrick and the one who picked up the phone when Jayson called. He wished the nigga would make up his mind. Did he want them to lay low or what? After getting knocked out by the lucky punch, Marley took no satisfaction in killing one of the niggas. He wanted them all dead, wanted immediate retaliation, but Jay didn't give him any info on the nigga that the original hit was out against. He simply told him to lay low. It wasn't the first time he bodied a nigga, but it was the first time he went into hiding. He felt like a real bitch. If he wasn't waiting on the $7,500 he was still owed, he would have bounced. There was something Jay was hiding from him. None of that really mattered to him. He hung up. "The nigga wants us to come to him in a spot called Altoona."

"Did he say he got our paper? I want to get back to the D," Trigger, whose real name was Wayne Holiday, asked. He also didn't feel the hiding out shit. "The nigga keep playing with my money, he can get it too."

Marley liked Trigger. The nigga thought like him. Always had. He'd been thinking along those lines himself. As they started to gather their belongings, he thought about it even more. If the nigga had thirty stacks to shell out, he had to have more. That's something he'd investigate after he got his remaining money he was owed. Marley didn't like the nigga much no ways. He was feeling his sister and the nigga acted like his sister was too good for him. After seeing Deamber, he questioned Jay about her. That's when the nigga acted like he wasn't good enough for her. After he dealt with Jay before he headed home, he'd holla at her—let her decide if he was good enough.

Trigger sat on the bed staring at Marley's sneaky ass. He knew immediately what the little smirk meant. The two met while both were serving time in a Michigan State Prison. They clicked instantly as cellmates. Over the months, they realized they had a lot in common. One night while wrestling playfully, Marley got behind Trigger attempting to slam him, when they fell to the bed with Marley on top of Trigger. It was that night that Marley engaged in his first homosexual encounter. For Trigger, it wasn't his first gay encounter, but it would be the first where he fell in love. Trigger was in the closet since his first gay encounter at fifteen. Before Marley, he went both ways. But over the years in prison and while out, he stopped sleeping with women. The same couldn't be said for Marley. He still fucked bitches. He wanted Jay's sister, and that was the reason for his smile. He was thinking about her.

If she was anywhere near her brother when they saw him, Trigger might kill her out of jealousy. No, he thought, he'd just fuck her and give her that hot shit. Trigger had gotten out of prison just six months ago, got out thinking it would be all good with him and Marley. Well, it wasn't all good. They shared an apartment, but nothing was the same. Marley acted like he didn't want anything to do with him. The only sex he got was to be allowed to give him an occasional blow job. He was ashamed. Trigger had no clue how to tell Marley he was HIV positive. He smiled as he plotted giving it to the bitch of Marley's desire.

"What you smiling at?"

"You," Trigger responded as he eyed Marley's naked chest.

Marley snatched up his tee and put it on. He hated when the nigga tried to act like a bitch. He wasn't gay or even bi. He got head from the nigga and hit him in his butt while in prison, but that was a done deal. The only reason why he hung out with him still was because Trigger had no fear. He killed with no remorse. He proved that in prison when he killed a nigga, and then the two niggas since he'd been out. "Get up and get dressed. He got a car coming for us." Before they got back to Detroit, he'd tell him that the faggot shit was over. Right now he was on some money shit. For awhile longer, he needed him.

It wasn't long before the hotel phone rang and the woman on the other end told him their limousine had arrived. He didn't think it was a real limo, but as soon as he saw the SUV style limo, his mind was made up. He'd see just how much more money Jay had. The nigga was obviously doing big things. As soon as the limo started to move, Marley stretched out. "Pour me a drink," he ordered. This was the style of living he could get used to, the kind of living he wanted. If he had to kill to achieve it, he'd do so easily. "Give me head, bitch!"

Trigger handed him his glass of Cognac and then unzipped his pants and took the dick he'd come to love into his mouth.

~ ~ ~

Back at the mansion, India removed Jayson's body. She didn't clean up the blood yet. There would soon be more blood on the floor. She'd have the entire room cleaned professionally. There was no way she'd be able to get all the blood up. "Are we clear on what I want done?"

"Absolutely!" Mr. Gary told her.

After watching his dogs in action, she didn't doubt him. She checked on her brother and Deamber. As she walked away from the room the two were in, she took out her cell phone, scrolled to the number she wanted, then pushed Send. The call was picked up on the third ring.

"Hello, India," the man on the other end said. He had long since programmed her number into his phone.

"You told me if I needed you for anything, to call. I'm calling."

~ ~ ~

As soon as Marley saw the mansion, his mind was made up. He knew Jayson was a dead man after he made him reveal where his stash was. "We gonna kill this nigga."

Trigger had already come to that conclusion.

The limo came to a stop and they both got out. As soon as he shut the door, he heard the locks engage. When they came out of the hotel, the man had been at the back door and opened and closed the door. Now the man hadn't even gotten out of the car. Marley's high instantly left him as he realized something was up. He reached for the gun he had in his waistband when they appeared.

Two pits jumped up on the car, and the other four encircled them, forcing them to put their backs onto the car.

He had a pit bull himself called Menace back in Detroit. He knew what a trained pit bull could do. He raised his hands straight up in the air. It was a setup and he was dumb enough to fall for it. He tried the handle on the door, already knowing it was locked.

"I wouldn't move another muscle if I was either of you."

The voice came from behind them, and neither turned their heads to see who spoke.

"Pretty sure you both know about pit bulls. My babies are not normal. They are trained to kill—not maim, bite, or injure," Mr. Gary advised as he advanced from behind them to stand just behind his dogs. "Keep your hands raised and step four steps away from the car." After they did as they were told, he walked behind them and removed their guns.

The whole time Marley looked for an opportunity get the upper hand on the old man. As long as the dogs had their eyes glued on them, he wouldn't attempt anything.

"Please follow me, and my dogs will bring up the rear." They followed him into the house and stepped into the racquetball court. "Someone will be with you two shortly."

In the room with the door shut, they both lowered their arms. They surveyed the court, saw the blood on the floor, and knew instantly that they had fucked up. Marley's mind began to race as he tried to think of a way out of his present situation. He was the first one to notice the woman headed down the hall toward them. At the glass that separated them, she stopped and stared at them. He couldn't stop himself from noticing her beauty. His hopes of getting out of his situation soared, and he smiled. Women couldn't stop from falling for him.

"Do either of you know who I am?"

He didn't, but he wouldn't mind getting to know her. "Never had the pleasure, sweetie."

"The fifteen-year-old boy one of you niggas killed was my baby brother," India revealed.

Marley lost his smile. "Sorry to hear that." He figured that they had Jayson somewhere and knew most if not the whole story. "Jayson hired us to kill a nigga. Your brother got hit by accident. It wasn't meant for him." That wasn't a lie. He really didn't give a fuck the young nigga was dead though. He wasn't about to reveal that though.

"In the center of that room you are standing in is Jayson's blood. And that was my other brother you two niggas were hired to kill."

The news wiped the confidence right out of their heads. Trigger heard all he needed to hear. He wasn't naive enough to think this woman went through so much trouble to have a powwow. They were as good as dead. At just twenty-five, he knew his days were numbered. He didn't have full-blown AIDS, but the prospect of living to an old man wasn't likely.

He was resigned to dying when the prison doctor told him he was HIV positive. He hadn't told Marley and there was no reason to tell him now. There was one thing he wanted to tell him. "I love you, Marley," he professed for the first time out loud.

When Trigger reached out attempting to embrace him, Marley pushed him roughly away, causing Trigger to stumble and nearly lose his balance.

"Don't you see this bitch is about to kill us?" Marley turned to look at India, who nodded her head up and down. "I didn't kill your brother," he lied. "He did." He pointed at Trigger.

Trigger, seeing Marley was turning against him, regained his footing and swung and connected two punches to the bigger and stronger nigga.

Caught off guard, Marley's lip split from the impact of the second punch. It didn't faze him. The punch he hit Trigger with sent him flying backward and then down to the floor, where he sat on his butt dazed. "He killed your brother, and I'll kill him if you let me go."

Trigger laughed as he spit out blood. "Let you go. I always knew you were more of a bitch than me. I should have been fucking your big soft ass in the butt instead of the other way around."

"Shut the fuck up!" he screamed. "He's lying," he said as he turned to look at India, as though she cared.

"Lying about you being a closet fag, hardly." Trigger slowly got to his feet. He ran his hands down his sides and rubbed his butt. "You loved fucking me in my ass, loved the way I sucked your little dick." He laughed again. "You want her to let you go for what, so you can live a long life? With what you got, I don't think so."

Marley turned in slow motion to face him. He caught on to the implications of his words, and his heart almost stopped.

"That's right. Found out while I was in prison that I'm HIV positive—my parting gift to you, baby."

Marley lost it at that point. He attacked Trigger, raining blows into his face.

Even after Trigger lost consciousness and blood ran out his nose, mouth, cuts, and ears, Marley didn't relent on his attack. He stood up and stomped on his head until it was misshapen and Trigger was dead. Brain matter and blood covered Marley's Timberland boots. His mind had snapped. HIV positive! He couldn't believe he had the hot shit.

India heard the exchange between the two, watching in awe as the enraged man killed his lover. She was glad she didn't allow the dogs to attack the two men. She didn't know if dogs could contract the virus and didn't want to take that chance.

LaRon came up to stand beside his sister. He looked at the scene on the court. "Both niggas got that hot shit. The one still living just found out." India pulled out her gun and opened up the door.

Marley stood over Trigger breathing heavily. "He's dead," he said simply. "He killed your brother and I killed him." He figured they were even.

India raised her hand and aimed at his chest. "I watched you pull the trigger. Go join your lover in hell." With that said, she pulled the trigger twice. Both bullets hit him in the chest and he fell. India reached out and grabbed her brother's arm when it looked like he was going to approach the niggas. "Too much contaminated blood, Bro. Before we go anywhere near them, we got to be completely covered."

He agreed with his sister. He didn't want to touch the gay-ass niggas. The bodies weren't going to move themselves. He followed his sister out.

After putting on several pairs of latex gloves, they set about putting the bodies in the coffins India purchased in preparation for the bodies that would fill them. When Marley moaned, they both jumped away from him.

LaRon pulled out his gun planning to finish what his sister started.

"Let him live. I got something special planned for him. He's the one that killed D," India said. She hadn't mentioned how she intended on getting rid of the bodies—just that she had a plan. She did mention that she'd be going to see Italian Mike at Rock Jungle.

Two hearses pulled up in front of the house. After loading the bodies, she returned to the house and took a quick shower. When she was dressed, she ran into Mr. Gary. She handed him the ten stacks she promised him. "Thank you, Mr. Gary."

He laughed as he pocketed the money. "I should be thanking you. Easiest money I ever made. If you ever need me or my babies again, I am just a phone call away. "

"Sounds good," she told him. Her original plan had the dogs tearing the niggas apart. That hot shit spoiled that.

Mr. Gary looked at India admiringly. "I'd hate to get on your bad side."

"I'd hate that too," she told him. She liked the old man. She followed him out the back to his truck.

"Load up," he ordered. All six dogs jumped up into the truck obediently. "Take care, young lady."

"You too." She watched him drive off and returned to the house.

"Am I following you?" LaRon asked.

"No. Take Deamber home. Take Jayson's car and leave yours here. Park it in the garage. You can get it later."

He hadn't done shit really. He didn't like not having more of a hand in the retaliation against his brother's killers. The only thing that stopped him is that his woman needed him. Truth be told, he needed her too. His best friend was in one of those coffins.

She could see her brother about to say something. "After I get rid of these bodies, I'll swing past. I'll handle things, LaRon."

He didn't doubt that. "Later."

She hugged him, hugged and kissed Deamber, and watched them drive off. After setting the alarm, she went to the drivers of the hearses. "Want y'all to follow me." In a small convoy, they headed back to Pittsburgh.

Back in Pittsburgh on the South Side, India had both hearses pull up at a gas station and fill up on gas. She took the opportunity to go talk to Mike. After explaining what she needed, she waited on his response.

"A place where these bodies will never be discovered? I just so happen to have a place that we could make that happen."

She knew her request was huge and wouldn't have blamed him if he said he couldn't help her. That he would and had a cemetery was a bonus. She would bury the nigga alive.

"Are the bodies close by?"

"Yes."

"Good. Have them follow us."

She stood along with him. "Where are we going?"

He couldn't get over how beautiful she was. "To Lawrenceville. I own a crematorium."

It was her turn to smile. It was perfect. "If you don't mind, I'll ride with you."

Mind? Hell, he would have insisted, come up with a lie to get her into his car. Her scent had him turned on. "That's fine. I'll bring you back here to your car."

"Great," she said as she allowed him to open the door for her and close it once she was seated.

With all three caskets lined up and with just the two of them in the crematory, Mike fired up the oven. "Nothing but ashes are left after this baby is done. There will be no bodies rising to the top of rivers. No one's dug up. Cyril Wecht won't be of no use once I'm done."

"That's the way I want it," she said. "Two of these men have HIV, so be careful when handling them."

He pulled out two sets of Teflon fire retardant gloves and a box of latex. "These will protect us. Soon the fire will be hot enough. Let's get this party started." He reached for a casket.

"Want that one to go last. Before we get started, can you get me a bucket of water?"

He thought it was a strange request, but he went off to do as she wanted.

Alone, she opened up Jayson's casket so she could look down on him. She couldn't believe he really had plotted to kill LaRon. The two were best friends. It went to show, when it came to money, family and friends meant little. She had to fight off the urge to cry.

Mike had no idea who the one she was looking down on was. He obviously meant something to her. He made more noise than he needed to, announcing he had returned. He sat the bucket of water down.

"I want to keep the ashes from this one."

"There's urns up front you can choose from. Put this over your mouth."

She took the mask he offered her and slipped it on. "You can do this one. I'll look at the urns." She didn't want to see Jayson go into the fire. She wasn't that strong. She left out, allowing Mike to put him on the conveyor belt himself.

When she returned ten minutes later, his body was still in the furnace. "It takes approximately twenty to twenty-five minutes to complete."

She stared at the furnace door in silence. Before she knew it, Mike pushed a button and the door opened. She took a few steps back to escape the heat coming out of the furnace.

By the time he had the third body on the conveyor belt, Mike was sweating and looking forward to a shower.

"Stand back," India said as she picked up the bucket of ice water. She hoped Murphy hadn't died yet and the water was enough to revive him. She dumped the water directly onto his face. When it brought little results, she hit him in his head with the bucket twice. He groaned.

Mike looked on in shock. He couldn't believe that the little fuck was still alive. "Wanted to torture him, but he has HIV. He's the one that killed my brother."

Marley wanted to get up. His skin on his back was peeling off due to the hotness of the steel slab he laid strapped to. His eyes bulged in fear and pain. The heat coming out the furnace burned the soles of his feet. His scream was weak, but filled with torment.

"This is a prelude to the hell where you'll spend eternity." She pushed the button, starting the conveyor belt moving.

His screams died out before his body entered the furnace fully.

Mike was ruthless, had killed men a number of ways in his rise to mob boss of Pittsburgh. He'd never done it in such a way before, nor had he witnessed such a brutal killing.

After it was all finished and the furnace was off, India asked, "Do I owe you anything Mike?"

He'd never met a woman quite like her. Black widow, that's what she was. But more than that, she intrigued him. How could someone be so absolutely gorgeous and be so deadly? "Glad to help."

He told her he'd have someone clean up and get rid of the caskets. That reminded her she had to return to Altoona and clean the racquetball court.

Back at her car, she shook Mike's hand and thanked him.

He drove off and she looked up at the clear cool night sky and smiled as she wiped away the tears that ran down her face. "It's over, lil Bro. I got them for you." She got into her car and pulled out her cell phone. "I'm on my way. It's done," she told LaRon. She hung up, vowing to herself as she drove toward her brother's home, that she'd never ever kill again.

She'd soon learn, never say never. What she thought was over was just the eye of the storm coming her way, to wreak havoc in her life and the lives of those she loved: her family. And that was something she would never allow!

EPILOGUE

Jocelyn straightened her grandson's bowtie for what seemed like the tenth time in the last hour. D.J., as he was now called, wasn't feeling the suit and tie he was forced to wear. At almost three years old, Jocelyn saw her son's swag in her grandson, as though they were one. "Touch it again so I can beat your little ass."

"It's choking me, Nanna."

"I'ma choke you if you touch it again. Mika, stop pulling at your dress." Her tomboy daughter was just as uncomfortable as her grandson. To get her in the dress wasn't an easy task.

George walked up and put his arm around her waist. "Breathe easy, baby." He knew better than to kiss her on her lips or cheek. Her handheld mirror would materialize and she'd do a touch-up.

Calming down was the last thing she was capable of at that moment. Today was the big day—the day she'd put so much time and effort into, to make it happen.

Everything had to be perfect. She owed it to her son. This was his dream.

Everyone breathed a sigh of relief when India came through the front doors carrying Desiree, Denean and Derrick's daughter. It meant everything was ready. "It's time," she announced.

Jocelyn pulled out the mirror and did a quick touch-up. She gave everyone the once over, took several deep breaths, and then outstretched her hands. A circle was made and everyone clasped hands. "Lord, I want to thank you for making this day possible. For without you, none of this would have been possible. When I get out there, give me the words to say. In Jesus name I pray. Amen."

"Amen!" everyone said.

"Let's go." She held onto D.J.'s hand as she led the way to the front door. Along with her were Denean, both her daughters, her two grandkids, LaRon, Deamber, and their two kids, Balil, India, and George and his twin daughters.

Michelle pushed open the door. The two friends and ex-crack friends hugged.

Both had come a long way. Since Derrick's death, Michelle had been a constant companion of Jocelyn's. Together the two had made this possible. It was only right that Michelle stood on the stage with them.

Thousands of people packed the parking lot, lined the sidewalks, and stood in the street. The section of Penn Avenue was closed off for the occasion. As soon as they stepped out, people began to cheer. The sound of the cheers was deafening. Every news station had an anchor covering the event. Cameras clicked as people used phones and cameras to record the event. The location where they stood used to be a Giant Eagle.

Long-time Garfield residents recalled the store being there, but it was vacant since it's closing in '86. It was an area that wasn't easy to purchase.

They waved as they headed up to the platform. The cheers got even louder as they stepped up to the podium and microphone.

Jocelyn had to wait for it to die down, which took five minutes. She lowered the mic to her height. "I want to thank you all for coming out today to join us in the grand opening of the Derrick Wright Recreation Center."

Two more minutes of cheering.

"As many of you know, my son was killed on his fifteenth birthday." She told herself she wouldn't cry, but someone obviously knew differently. A box of Kleenex was on the podium. She pulled several out and dabbed at the corners of her eyes. "I'm sorry. He was still a child. Just two years into his teens. Way too young to die. Yet, this has become a common occurrence in far too many inner city neighborhoods. Not only in our city, but in most cities across the country. The sad thing is black males under twenty-five are faring the worst. Boys not growing up to be men. Young girls not reaching womanhood. Struck down before they truly know what life is about. My friend Michelle standing here beside me lost her daughter Kelly, who was just sixteen, to violence. No parent should ever have to bury their child. And oftentimes the killer turns out to be another young black male. It's a vicious cycle that is destroying our communities. Watching my son's casket be lowered into the ground was the worst and hardest time of my life."

She paused, having to get her emotions together. A lot of people listening wiped away at their own tears. "Before my son passed, we sat one morning in our dining room and talked. This was before we moved from Cornwall Street. It was right after Kelly was killed. I sat him down and asked him what he planned on doing with his life. It was then when he told me about wanting a place where kids could go not only to have fun, but to learn. He was taken away from me before he made his dreams a reality. Today it gives me great pleasure to introduce the Derrick Wright Recreation Center."

Two doves were released, along with 5,475 balloons, equaling the days he had on earth. The cheers this time mingled in with shouts of "We love you, D."

It was a day they looked forward to. Michelle was the one that cut the huge red ribbon, allowing people inside for the first time.

Everyone standing in attendance wasn't there to join in the

festivities. Clyde Dexter, now a detective in the Narcotics Division, stood amongst the crowd. His job assignment deemed it necessary for him to be there. His eyes continued to travel and linger on India. She was still a beautiful woman. Originally, he hoped he'd be able to solve the murder case involving her brother, but it was moved to unsolved. Seeing her now he realized he was still drawn to her. Many nights her face invaded his dreams. He considered himself a normal black male, a year from age thirty. He was relatively handsome, didn't have any problems getting women. Had a couple in the time since he first laid eyes on her. But none compared to her beauty. What messed him up more than that was the real fact that he was in love with her. They'd not been on one date, held hands, nothing. He couldn't help but feel guilty about the assignment he was on—to take down the city's biggest drug dealer. And that dealer happened to be none other than LaRon Jones, her brother.

He didn't like meeting her after the death of one brother, only to re-enter her life by taking down another, but it was his job—the biggest of his career. Could he do it knowing it would mess up any chance of him having India? He didn't have a choice. He looked at her again, and it looked like she looked at him as well.

India was hands-on at the rec center. Every day after attending her last year of college classes, she made it there to help out. After just two weeks, the center was already considered a huge success. A similar center that would bear Kelly's name was already in the beginning stages of opening in Homewood. Although India had always wanted to be an attorney, her involvement gave her satisfaction. Seeing the smiles on the kids' faces daily was priceless.

"Ms. India, some man named Isaac Newton wants to see you," Angela said. Angela was one of the many teens volunteering at the center. She attended Peabody High School and was a senior.

India was in her office when the girl knocked lightly on her open door. She looked up and smiled. "Have you decided on a college?"

That she was even going to college was a miracle in itself. If she hadn't met India, she knew that never would have happened. With a one-year-old son that she was raising on her own, Angie had dropped out. When she showed up at the rec center looking for a job, she met India. After talking, she got more than a job. She got a mentor and friend. She returned to school, attended summer school, and now was caught up and would be graduating with her class. Her SAT scores were high enough to get her some scholarship offers. India had promised Angie her son would be cared for while she was away at college. She had no family that weren't effected by drugs. Her grandmother, at the age of sixty-two, offered to help, but India thought the old woman deserved to enjoy her retirement years. "Not yet, but I think I'm staying here." She didn't think she could go weeks without her son.

"Okay, if you need anything, don't hesitate to ask. Send him in." Angie went to get the man.

"India," Isaac said as he stepped into the office.

Angie closed the door and India stood and shook the investigator's hand. "I located them."

Her long search for her sisters spanned across state lines and back again. Her father said his two youngest kids were in Pennsylvania. Originally, they were, but they moved to Nevada, Jersey, New York, and then back to Pennsylvania.

Philadelphia is where Isaac had just returned from. It had taken her so long to locate them, causing her a lot of anxiety and sleepless nights. The news weakened her knees and she had to sit down. Isaac would walk across lava to please India.

He could have sent one of his investigators, but decided to make the trip to Philly on his own. What awaited him there would no doubt break her heart.

"Don't sugarcoat anything." She could see from his expression he had some bad news.

"India, I'm sorry. Your sisters have had a horrible life up to this point." He went on telling her everything he learned on his trip.

His words brought tears to her eyes. She couldn't believe what she heard. "India, just say the word and I'll get on it." He was willing to kill for her.

She gathered herself and wiped her tears. "Thank you, but I'll handle it." She accepted the folder he extended toward her.

She gave him a check for $75,000, the agreed upon amount.

After he left, India sat alone in her office letting it all soak in. Two pictures of both her sisters with their names under them were taped to the inside of the folder. She ran her finger across their beautiful faces, as though she was actually caressing them. Carla and Sandra, "I'm coming for y'all," she vowed. And whoever hurt them and forced them into the situation they were in would pay with their lives. It was her responsibility to protect them. Since an early age, she put in her own work. It didn't stop yet and it probably never would. India was going to get her sisters.

To be continued . . .

Text Good2Go at 31996 to receive new release updates via text message.

COMING SOON

The Flip Side

The story picks up with India locating her lost sisters—a joyous occasion that soon puts her and those that she loves in a fight for their freedom and lives, as they now must face the flip side of the game . . .

To order books, please fill out the order form below:
To order films please go to **www.good2gofilms.com**

Name:_____

Address:_____

City: _____ State: _____ Zip Code: _____

Phone:_____

Email:_____

Method of Payment: Check   VISA   MASTERCARD

Credit Card#:_____

Name as it appears on card: _____

Signature: _____

Item Name	Price	Qty	Amount
48 Hours to Die – Silk White	$14.99		
A Hustler's Dream - Ernest Morris	$14.99		
A Hustler's Dream 2 - Ernest Morris	$14.99		
Bloody Mayhem Down South	$14.99		
Business Is Business – Silk White	$14.99		
Business Is Business 2 – Silk White	$14.99		
Business Is Business 3 – Silk White	$14.99		
Childhood Sweethearts – Jacob Spears	$14.99		
Childhood Sweethearts 2 – Jacob Spears	$14.99		
Childhood Sweethearts 3 - Jacob Spears	$14.99		
Childhood Sweethearts 4 - Jacob Spears	$14.99		
Connected To The Plug – Dwan Marquis Williams	$14.99		
Connected To The Plug 2 – Dwan Marquis Williams	$14.99		
Deadly Reunion – Ernest Morris	$14.99		
Flipping Numbers – Ernest Morris	$14.99		
Flipping Numbers 2 – Ernest Morris	$14.99		
He Loves Me, He Loves You Not - Mychea	$14.99		
He Loves Me, He Loves You Not 2 - Mychea	$14.99		
He Loves Me, He Loves You Not 3 - Mychea	$14.99		
He Loves Me, He Loves You Not 4 – Mychea	$14.99		
He Loves Me, He Loves You Not 5 – Mychea	$14.99		
Lord of My Land – Jay Morrison	$14.99		
Lost and Turned Out – Ernest Morris	$14.99		
Married To Da Streets – Silk White	$14.99		
M.E.R.C. - Make Every Rep Count Health and Fitness	$14.99		
Money Make Me Cum – Ernest Morris	$14.99		
My Besties – Asia Hill	$14.99		

My Besties 2 – Asia Hill	$14.99		
My Besties 3 – Asia Hill	$14.99		
My Besties 4 – Asia Hill	$14.99		
My Boyfriend's Wife - Mychea	$14.99		
My Boyfriend's Wife 2 – Mychea	$14.99		
My Brothers Envy – J. L. Rose	$14.99		
My Brothers Envy 2 – J. L. Rose	$14.99		
Naughty Housewives – Ernest Morris	$14.99		
Naughty Housewives 2 – Ernest Morris	$14.99		
Naughty Housewives 3 – Ernest Morris	$14.99		
Naughty Housewives 4 – Ernest Morris	$14.99		
Never Be The Same – Silk White	$14.99		
Stranded – Silk White	$14.99		
Slumped – Jason Brent	$14.99		
Supreme & Justice – Ernest Morris	$14.99		
Tears of a Hustler - Silk White	$14.99		
Tears of a Hustler 2 - Silk White	$14.99		
Tears of a Hustler 3 - Silk White	$14.99		
Tears of a Hustler 4- Silk White	$14.99		
Tears of a Hustler 5 – Silk White	$14.99		
Tears of a Hustler 6 – Silk White	$14.99		
The Panty Ripper - Reality Way	$14.99		
The Panty Ripper 3 – Reality Way	$14.99		
The Solution – Jay Morrison	$14.99		
The Teflon Queen – Silk White	$14.99		
The Teflon Queen 2 – Silk White	$14.99		
The Teflon Queen 3 – Silk White	$14.99		
The Teflon Queen 4 – Silk White	$14.99		
The Teflon Queen 5 – Silk White	$14.99		
The Teflon Queen 6 - Silk White	$14.99		
The Vacation – Silk White	$14.99		
Tied To A Boss - J.L. Rose	$14.99		
Tied To A Boss 2 - J.L. Rose	$14.99		

Tied To A Boss 3 - J.L. Rose	$14.99		
Tied To A Boss 4 - J.L. Rose	$14.99		
Tied To A Boss 5 - J.L. Rose	$14.99		
Time Is Money - Silk White	$14.99		
Tomorrow's Not Promised	$14.99		
Two Mask One Heart – Jacob Spears and Trayvon Jackson	$14.99		
Two Mask One Heart 2 – Jacob Spears and Trayvon Jackson	$14.99		
Two Mask One Heart 3 – Jacob Spears and Trayvon Jackson	$14.99		
Wrong Place Wrong Time – Silk White	$14.99		
Young Goonz – Reality Way	$14.99		
Subtotal:			
Tax:			
Shipping (Free) U.S. Media Mail:			
Total:			

Make Checks Payable To:
Good2Go Publishing
7311 W Glass Lane,
Laveen, AZ 85339

CPSIA information can be obtained
at www.ICGtesting.com
Printed in the USA
LVHW01s0243191117
556879LV00001B/9/P